THE CASE WORKER

George Konrad

Translated by Paul Aston

Hutchinson
London Melbourne Sydney Auckland Johannesburg

Hutchinson & Co. (Publishers) Ltd
An imprint of the Hutchinson Publishing Group
24 Highbury Crescent, London N5 1RX

Hutchinson Group (Australia) Pty Ltd
30–32 Cremorne Street, Richmond South, Victoria 3121
PO Box 151, Broadway, New South Wales 2007

Hutchinson Group (NZ) Ltd
32–34 View Road, PO Box 40–086, Glenfield, Auckland 10

Hutchinson Group (SA) (Pty) Ltd
PO Box 337, Bergvlei 2012, South Africa

First published in Great Britain 1975
First published in a paperback edition 1977
Reprinted 1979, 1981

© George Konrad 1975

Printed in Great Britain by The Anchor Press Ltd
and bound by Wm Brendon & Son Ltd
both of Tiptree, Essex

ISBN 0 09 131701 0

THE CASE WORKER

RULES AND
REGULATIONS

Go on, I say to my client. Out of habit, because I can guess what he's going to say, and doubt his truthfulness. He complains some more, justifies himself, puts the blame on others. From time to time he bursts into tears. Half of what he says is beside the point; he reels off platitudes, he unburdens himself. He thinks his situation is desperate; seems perfectly normal to me. He swears his cross is too heavy; seems quite bearable to me. He hints at suicide; I let it pass. He thinks I can save him; I can't tell him how wrong he is.

From time to time his face changes; one expression is superimposed on another. First the features are flaccid, then they organize themselves around the bony structure. The first face is already forgotten, the second might still arouse some interest. A network of blood vessels and fatty cysts, dilated pores, liver spots, and pimples form a relief map; swelling and receding surfaces, angular, arched, or flattened furrows, unfinished wrinkles add up to a cryptogram that has defied every attempt to solve it. Bewildered eyes may have studied every bit of this landscape with greater passion, but I have the advantage of objectivity. We are at once enemies and accomplices; I, his contemporary, am closer to this man than his descendants will be—cold death masks, dwellers in nothingness. Ill at ease, but with the authority of routine, I run my eye over this sketch of the future, my client's face.

2

To the left of my desk in my fourth-floor office, a double window opens out on a narrow, enclosed courtyard. The offices are connected by circular outside corridors. A strong wind has been blowing for several days, drawing a trail of smoke down from the chimney, across the railings of the corridors, and down into the concrete yard, littered with oil drums and iron bars. For a moment the trail straightens out to form tall, angry pillars, then falls back again into the trough delimited by the stairwell and the four walls. The smoke screen blunts the contours of our four-story column of emptiness. This is our world; the lights of our windows blink at each other, doors bang erratically, clients clutch the high stair rail; and here we are, encapsulated in this uninspiring shell, this monument to the social order, where every morning for the past ten years—God knows why—I have snuggled down as if into bed. The smoke screen lifts again, and between the upper window frame and the ridge of the roof opposite, I can see a patch of sky, traversed by the fleeting white trail of a jet fighter high above the city.

3

An old woman came to the building to apply for supplementary benefits. She had no pension and no relatives to turn to. When she reached the heavy iron door, she was unable to open it because the superintendent had fitted it with a new, strong inside spring. From his glass cage the porter, his neck encased in a metal brace, watched the old woman emerge from the opaque curtain of snow, but then, as usual, he closed his eyes again because the light hurt his inflamed lids. The old woman lost heart, went home, and hanged herself from a curtain rod. Before doing so, she wrote a letter to the management explaining that it had been impossible to open the door, and requesting that her possessions be turned over to her miserly son. The director was furious and scolded the superintendent, who instructed the fitters to put in another spring. A month later this was done. Until then the iron door from the street squeaked abominably and slammed on the heels of everyone who came in. It took a certain adroitness to slip through in time, for the door snapped back mercilessly on any slow-moving arrival. The elderly employees would wait outside until a more vigorous colleague came along and helped them through to the flesh-colored, imitation-marble lobby. As for me, I managed to tame this noisy, churlish contraption.

4

I can't abide the entrance or the lobby with its smell of cauliflower. On the wall, notices from the probate court call on the heirs of deceased elderly persons to come and take possession of their chattels. As part of my responsibilities, I have to catalogue inheritances. It's dirty work, but at least there's a certain musty intimacy about it. The names on the notices—my eye lights on them in spite of me—savor quaintly of the past. They evoke lumpy walnut beds, muted grandfather clocks, carving knives worn thin by constant sharpening, slippers grown cold, and the timeless smile of family photographs in gilt frames—the pallid futility of objects left ownerless and reduced to junk.

The imitation marble on my right belongs to the dead, while the glass cage opposite it belongs to the porter with the steel-encased neck. Every morning he blinks benevolently at each new arrival, because for many years he has been unable to nod. Only once does he stand up, when the director arrives; then he murmurs words of greeting from his booth and taps on the glass with his crippled hand. The director taps back and gives him an encouraging smile. Enriched by this perfunctory smile, the porter is quite happy to sit in silence for the rest of the day until the director leaves at five. Of the two noteworthy events of the day, one is already behind him. But at one o'clock he has to shut the outside door and make it clear to ordinary members of the public who rattle at the door that from then on they have no possible business in the building outside of office hours. The would-be clients are often obstreperous—it's their nature, and you can hardly blame them; they need something, and that makes them importunate and slow to get the message. Consequently, a surly grimace or wave of the hand won't always do it; sometimes the porter has to open his mouth: "Tomorrow, I said! No exceptions." But if a government official approaches, the old mechanized neck takes in at a glance the air of easy assurance that distinguishes persons with official business from those obstinately pursuing their private affairs. On such occasions he opens the door with the promptness of a photoelectric

6

cell, though he does not always return the greeting. The old curmudgeon will soon be moving from his glass cage to the imitation marble across the way. I asked him not long ago if he had made his will. He said he had plenty of time; besides, he had no relatives and he'd like best for his belongings to be burned along with him.

5

One compartment of my filing cabinet is full of miscellaneous unofficial mementos. Among other things, I have piously preserved (though not for their rarity) certain proofs of man's inventiveness. A whip with three lashes, a bamboo stick filled with lead, a miniature pillory—all homemade. These implements were employed by fathers and mothers; maybe they didn't actually derive any pleasure from them, but one day (they kept repeating) the child would be grateful for their severity.

There are also photographs in my filing cabinet. One shows a spruce old man; standing on a chair with his pants down, he is blowing kisses out the window and smiling benignly. Across the street there was a school for retarded children; one of the women teachers photographed him from a window. I was there when they brought him in for questioning. At first I took him for a common exhibitionist, but later it turned out that he had practiced his sexual perversions on a dozen or more mentally retarded boys and girls. The children came to the hearing with their parents, who flung themselves at the old man in the corridor, as he was being brought in from the detention cell. Three hefty detectives saved him from being lynched. In the interrogation room he wept, threw himself face down on the floor, and whimpered about the brutality of his interrogators. Actually, I felt rather sorry for him, and asked the detectives to treat him more gently. The same day he had a hemorrhage, and the judge released him on probation. When he recovered he went to the city park and strangled a child who had run away from home. I'm told that he crossed the prison yard on his way to the gallows smiling amiably and stroking his neck, but that he collapsed at the sight of the ladder. Two minutes before the sentence could be carried out, he died of heart failure.

Another item in my collection is a tape recording. If you ran it off you'd hear a radio playing muffled dance music, girls screaming, the sound of struggling bodies, matter-of-fact voices urging them on. Some bored teen-agers had wanted to immortalize the memorable half hours they had spent with a group of grade-school girls. With one exception, all the girls submitted to rape, and some even returned voluntarily to the scene of their downfall. One of them said later: "At first it was kind of nasty, but after a while it felt good. Whenever I got bored, I'd go up to Little Arab's place; three boys at once, you see, is more interesting than just one. At least there was something doing." In prison, Little Arab's mind became unhinged, his memory deserted him, he swallowed spoons, and the guards were kept busy forcing boiled potatoes down his throat. Then he was transferred to an iron-barred bunk in the "loony bin," where he spends his days exchanging ineptitudes with his fellow inmates.

Then there's a childish drawing entitled "The Massacre of the Ghosts." A ten-year-old boy drew it on the corner of my table the day I took him to an institution. A crowd of hooded ghosts are jostling each other in the innards of a whale with a huge tooth-studded mouth. A dense mob of children are shooting arrows at them. At the exit of one of the intestinal tunnels lies a little figure with arms outspread, above it the caption; "This is me, Laci. I know you won't avenge me." Laci died a year ago. He ran away from the institution, and in the course of his half-conscious wanderings tried to scale the sheer rock face of Gellért Hill.

He had almost reached the top when he fell. About my avenging him, he was right; I didn't take much action against the hooded ghosts.

Lastly, a dusty braid of gray hair, tied with a golden ribbon, and a card bearing the plaintive message: "In memory of old Karola, who is preparing to meet her Maker and who for the last five years has been pleading vainly with Mr. —— to leave the flock of black sheep and join the white flock of our Saviour."

It was I who had placed Karola in custody. This she resented, and often came to my office in the hope of converting me. She would read me her depressingly long religious poems, beaming at me as she waited for compliments. Many times I resolved to throw her out, but in the end I always covered her with praises.

The other day I went to her funeral, which came at the same time as that of a colleague. Her sisters in faith, the white lambs, sang hymns over her open grave. These beady-eyed old ladies smelled of airless rooms and evidently disapproved of Karola's evangelist excesses. Even the pastor was displeased at the hymn singing, which he thought out of place. A young man wearing dark glasses clicked away with his camera; he brought me a picture of the modestly flowered grave. This and a photograph of my colleague's funeral have their place side by side with the braid.

From the depths of memory, snatches of the farewell speeches delivered beside my colleague's bier still come back to me: the eloquent phrases selected from published collections of funeral orations, classified according to the age, sex, and rank of the deceased. One after the other, in the order of their importance, the wretchedly paid speakers—first from our department, then from the greater and lesser institutions and organizations—came forward, and with their backs to the mourners, addressed themselves to the departed. Dressed in his Sunday best, his jaws closed for good, he lay in the black-draped mortuary chapel cluttered with white wreaths, presenting his mortal remains, which had been transferred from the morgue, to the assembled mourners. In a semicircle around the lauded and lamented corpse stood the jostling, stagestruck choir. The horizontal rays of the afternoon sun cast a farewell glow on the choirmaster's sweating nape. Gaping, nicotine-stained teeth chewed resolutely away at the limp stanzas of the dirge, in which shroud, banner, glorious struggle, and illustrious example were duly mentioned. The mourners facing the choir mumbled with immobile lips. Helped on its way by top-hatted undertaker's assistants, the coffin rumbled over greased runners into the hearse. Greedy glances came to rest on the widow's tear-soaked face. And when, at the end of the rather protracted ceremony, a temporary wooden marker was put at the head of the still fresh mound in the churchyard, the director's hand described an elegant arc and descended on the old woman's hand, which was clutching its damp handkerchief. He gave it a mild, almost boyish pat: We must be brave, if you have any problems don't hesitate . . . On soft springs, the director's black car vanished into the dusk; the unmotorized mourners drifted off to various bars, the wind buffeted the smoke rising from burning leaves in nearby backyards, hysterical cats scuttled over the gravel, shutters rattled. Stale laughter hovers in the doorway of the café. Inside, the smell of Riesling and fried sausages; flat feet are resting, death is cloistered, the office will be open all day tomorrow, enormous backlog. My colleague will eat no more sausages, but then he will have no more baffling cases to worry about, no more mail to sort, no clients to listen to. Never again will he have to disentangle requests, complaints, and recriminations from ponderous sentences disjointed by interjections, make the right decision, and record it, couched in the accepted circumlocutory jargon, on dotted lines. His haughty mask is

10

now preserved only in the photograph the young man snapped for me at a reasonable price and which now lies here in my filing cabinet with the rest of my unofficial odds and ends.

6

The other filing cabinet stands in the center of the plaster wall. With its doors wide open it makes me think of an old man holding open his dressing gown so the doctor can examine his abdomen. Every morning I reach with sickening pity into this ancient object, where three rows of case histories, filed according to date and category, await decisions. Now and then they are removed, stapled to sheets of background information, refiled under new reference numbers, sent for consideration to other offices, and returned dog-eared and covered with endless scribblings. And here they lie.

I sometimes wonder what would happen if suddenly they were to start talking. What sounds would issue from that cabinet! Children's cries, women's moans, resounding blows, quarrels, obscenities, recriminations, interrogations, hasty decisions, false testimony, administrative platitudes, jovial police slang, judges' verdicts, the vapid chatter of female supervisors, the incantations of psychologists, my colleagues' embittered humor, my own solitary invective, and so on and so on. It would be as if a powerful radio had picked up all the stations in the world at once; all these sounds, en masse, would become as neutral and indifferent as the yellowing documents in my drawers.

Each file starts out with a petition, a complaint, or denunciation, continues with a summons and a police report, and ends with a judgment. Following a trajectory traced by the legal and administrative code, it rises high above the original lowly offense into a rarefied atmosphere

11

that sparkles with procedural subtleties. Frankly, it gives me no great pleasure to see my files departing with an elegant leap from the seething human life that gave rise to them, and I must admit to a certain malicious pleasure when, after the showy acrobatics of official procedure, they crash land in my filing cabinet. But sometimes my compassion with one or another of these files resembles the pity a dramatist must feel when his obstinate hero takes a fall: he endows him with every possible advantage— from the pure motives and trenchant rhetoric of the true moralist who aims to correct the faulty nature of things, to the passion that ennobles the trivialities of life—and comes to grief all the same. With a stroke of the surgical knife it might be possible to cut short the propagation of human weaknesses; but, just as a living body rejects alien matter, so everyday life evacuates all peremptory regulations, cozily dogmatic verdicts—in a word, everything that is strictly logical and consistent—and then proceeds to solve its problems by quiet trickery and always in the most unexpected way. Which accounts for the fate of my pitiful, cruel, and sometimes rather ridiculous documents.

7

If I sit at my desk with my head in my hands, it is because the moment I entered the office a thousand pygmy typewriters began to clatter right and left, hurling incongruous phrases into the ever shrinking field of my attention . . .

if a few drops of brandy make my nerves pulsate as an electric current awakens a dusty old television set to life, my benumbed brain starts crackling and, liberated from the insufferable hammering, engenders images that, at first diffuse, then organized, parade across my hesitant retina . . .

if nobody says anything; if the telephone keeps quiet, the radiator doesn't hiss, the loudspeaker doesn't bark, the door of the elevator doesn't clatter every minute, and diarrheal pigeons are not scratching at my windowsill; if the worn-down shoes of uncertain, nosy people are not shuffling past my window . . .

if from my memory that is becoming more and more like a junk pile I expel table-pounding ministers of war, official spokesmen who communicate nothing, mass murderers dozing in bulletproof docks, double agents exchanged on the q.t., newly spawned popular dictators who string up their friends, cannibalistic monarchs by divine right, the season's celebrities whose electronic smile invades every room, who unveil statues, taste the new wine, inaugurate highways, inspect guards of honor, kiss babies, send telegrams of congratulation, and present medals and gold watches . . .

if my wife and I have gone for our usual quiet walk on the hillside the night before; if the rent, electric, and telephone bills have been paid and there's still enough money for milk, meat, fruit, coffee, tobacco, and wine . . .

if after a good night's sleep, propelled to the washbasin by the exploding alarm, I have successfully completed the befuddled ritual of getting up; if with the aroma of fresh coffee in my head I have managed, on taking the bus, to find a seat by the window and collect my thoughts amid overcoats smelling of tobacco, rain, dishwater, and dry toast . . .

. . . then, even then, this day will be still pretty much the same as every other day.

8

My clients in the waiting room are making more and more of a hubbub. They kick the standing ashtray, fiddle with the squeaking radiator valve, cough, clear their throats, speculate on the outcome of their visits. Every day without fail they are here; if they could, they'd come on Sunday as well. The faces change, the grievances are always pretty much the same. If nothing else, they derive a certain perverse pleasure in having their complaints officially recorded. How natural that they should come and demand attention. As long as this building stands, clients will come here to take up some official's morning hours and entertain him with their problems. Since a client has worries, he is defenseless. By the time he reaches the inner office, the wait, his plight, and his sense of guilt have shaken his confidence. The bare gray walls, the dreary regulation furniture, the colorless faces of the office staff, the clack of typewriters filtering through from neighboring offices, and the mutterings of those behind him in the line bring him face to face with himself. The official, on the other hand, has nothing to worry about. Impassive, draped in condescending superiority, he has the client—that frail, flustered being who wants something or is afraid of something—admitted. If the official had cares of his own, he himself would degenerate into a client in some other office, on the other side of just such a desk. The standard desk is no more than a yard deep. But the two persons facing each other across it are as far apart as convict and jailer on opposite sides of the bars. There is no way around or across this desk; it stands between two faces, two enigmas, inert, but apportioning the roles as unmistakably as a whipping post or a guillotine.

Ill at ease, the client remains standing until offered a chair; nervously he fiddles with a cigarette, and eventually asks for permission to light it. His sweat glands operate at full capacity, his breath goes sour, the blood rises to his forehead. Finally, after beating about the bush for a while, he delivers himself of confessions that close friends would hesitate to make to each other. Since there are no counterconfessions to distract him, the floor is all his. Even a civil servant, silently smoking amid bleak official furniture, can serve as confessor. He leans forward attentively and asks two or three expert questions; that suffices to release the flood. The questioner must proceed as delicately as a surgeon probing with his scalpel or a mother resting a soothing hand on her child's bellyache. In a calm, workaday voice he dwells on unlikely details, remarking from time to time: "Unfortunate . . . that wasn't nice of him . . . yes, I see . . . that was bad . . ." At the same time he tries to avoid the pitfalls of unguarded commiseration, expressing mild disapproval of the client's weakness, but also evincing professional skepticism. In the presence of routine cases he may show a certain boredom, while extreme cases arouse his scientific enthusiasm. The client vanishes behind his case, the official behind his function. Meanwhile, the case in three of four copies thunders over the typewriter, which tinkles at the end of each line and finally delivers itself of the formula: "The witness wishes to add nothing further to his statement and signs it herewith. Date as above."

At the beginning of my career, I thought: It's like swallowing fistfuls of mud; I can neither digest it nor vomit it up. In the last ten years I must have said, "Have a seat, please," thirty thousand times. Apart from colleagues, witnesses, informers, prying newspapermen, and a few inoffensive mental cases, it was distress that drove most of them to my desk. In most instances their anguish was massive, tentacular, and incurable; it weighed on me in this room where people cry, "Believe me, it hurts," "I can't go on," and "It's killing me," as easily as they would scream on a roller coaster. On the whole, my interrogations make me think of a surgeon who sews up his incision without removing the tumor.

Every institution makes for a specific state of mind. At the circus my client laughs, at the public baths he day-

15

dreams, on the streetcar he stares into space, at a boxing match he is aggressive, in the cemetery subdued, and so on. To this room he brings a few samples of his sufferings and of frustrations that he has handed on to his sons and daughters. Quite possibly the image I get—the barest tip of the fragile molehill of his life—is deceptive. Yesterday he was kicked, today he gets apologies and tomorrow he may even come in for a caress or two, but all I see is his past. Nevertheless, I trust the momentary image, though with some caution. I may not know the man himself, but I know his circumstances. A diagram of his blunders, superimposed on those of other people, brings out what is specific to him, showing that what is unpredictable in him is infinitesimal compared to what is predictable. His circumstances are, let us say, straitened. In my official capacity I am informed of his job, habits, and previous blunders; this allows me to estimate how much freedom of action he has. Of course, what I see isn't the man himself, but only the envelope in which he moves about. Yet, reluctantly, I identify my client with all these odds and ends, and feel sorry for him because so many obstacles have impeded his development. It would be commendable if his relations with his environment were somewhat more complex, if the rules he chose to live by were a little less conventional. But his system is depressingly lacking in complexity, his income wretched, his physical surroundings dreary, his vision blurred, his burden heavy. His freedom of action is below average, his drives, which are without direction, conflict and sometimes collide head on. When this happens, the traffic jams up and official intervention is needed to start it moving again. Since my job is to protect children and safeguard the interests of the state, the most I can do is reconcile him with his circumstances and oppose his propensity for suffering. I do what the law and my fumbling judgment permit; then I look on, mesmerized, as the system crushes him.

9

I spent six months of my military service in an engineer squad, clearing mine fields. All around us the world was at peace, but we were at war. It wasn't just the money, the oranges, and the chocolate that appealed to us, or even the pride in belonging to a special unit. We were also attracted by what was virtually a game of chance. Every morning, though of course we took every precaution, we diced with death. Laden with our mine-detector equipment, we crawled about, caressing the ground as gingerly as a neophyte lion tamer caresses the great beast's neck. Even under the vertical rags of the sun the marshy woods were bottle green; fat dragonflies sunned themselves on the off-white skulls of a German armored brigade. We besieged those skeletons for months. A double ring of mines surrounded them, one that they themselves had laid and another planted by the Russians, who, having no time to waste, had merely doubled the invisible barrier and gone off through the woods, leaving the obstinate brigade to starvation and to the birds of the air. We had no idea of the pattern of either ring; the secret lay with the victorious dead and the defeated dead. In any case, it was an insane, hastily improvised scheme, impossible to figure out; all we could do was grope our way amid the blind spirits of the sinister forest, wondering whether there would be as many of us at lunch as when we had gone out in the morning. Perhaps because everyone else was at peace, we looked on the constant possibility of a sudden explosion as a fair sporting risk. As, freshly shaven, we sipped our afternoon coffee, we would imagine that our fingers were touching the invisible copper wires, taut to the point of snapping, that maintained the detonators of the mines that might still await us in a provisional state of quiescence.

At that time unpleasant things were also happening at

home: a brother of one of the men in the squad was hanged, another's father was beaten till he was half dead, the families of some had merely been resettled or interned, while those of others had not been molested. It was no more possible to see where these lightnings would strike than which of our mines, to which we referred by charming female names, might explode. This work is cleaner, one of us said, and we agreed with him. Cleaner than what? None of us asked this pertinent question.

We were all demobilized long ago and have had children by the first woman at hand. "I'll be home at five-thirty," we say in the morning, and usually make it by a quarter to six; our clients don't shoot, the files don't explode, and no strangers with badges under their lapels grab us by the arms in the street. Even so, what was true then is still true today. It was cleaner working on our bellies in the marshy forest, trying to decipher the hieroglyphic pattern of those murderous devices which separated us from the bared bones of the Germans and had outlived the men who laid them, cleaner than sitting in white cuffs trying to defuse mines that have ticked away for years and that one false move can suddenly detonate—civilian mines skulking in memories, in beds, in words and fists. You don't even notice them, but some day their delayed action will blow someone up. Tomorrow? In ten years? Don't be impatient, you'll find out one of these days—when it's too late to do anything about it.

SUICIDE CASES

Suicides have been giving me a lot of work lately. Abandoning home, hearth, and work, they plunge into the silence that knows no suffering. They depart in haste, mysteriously, as though to take the long trip. Of every hundred deaths, statisticians say, ninety-seven are unintentional, three voluntary. Of all nations, mine has the highest suicide rate. Does that make it the freest? Its freedom, I believe, goes hand in hand with the angels of corruption and failure.

Each year, one in every thousand of my fellow countrymen tries to cancel himself out. What does this one case matter? And why should it matter to me that in the crowd going and coming around me, gathering on sidewalks, in buses, shops, and cafés, finally to disperse at night and take refuge behind alien walls, one in a thousand will most probably, some time this year, take poison, drink lye, string himself up, throw himself under a bus, slash his wrists, jump out of the window, blow his brains out, or hurl himself into the Danube? We don't know him and don't want to; he is undoubtedly unbalanced. All we feel is disgust, barely tinged with pity. The cowardly, black-mailing, opportunistic clown. Doesn't like our company, eh? Thinks we'll miss him, does he? All right, good-bye and good riddance. We'll be hanging on a little longer, maybe five or ten thousand years.

There's a nurse I know: when wailing ambulances bring in unsuccessful suicide cases to get their stomachs pumped, she takes them to the toilet and beats them up. I used to think her attitude was perverse. Not any more. I've seen it often enough—even someone who loved him will often light into an unsuccessful suicide. Human solidarity de-crees that it's better to kill a man than to let him demon-strate his originality by doing the job himself.

It is not easy pity but my professional obligations that have involved me with these cases. If a suicide leaves minor children or if he himself is a minor, I have to draw up a file on his death. I am obliged by law to investigate, make decisions, and take action; this compels me, like it or not, to take an interest, not perhaps in the manner of their pass-ing—which is usually quite conventional—but at least in the life that has thus come to an end. And even more so if it has not come to an end: if their stomachs have been pumped or their wounds stitched up, if they have been dragged out of the gas-filled kitchen or cut down from the rope—in short, if they have been rescued in time. Alive or dead, I must, in considering their cases, bear in mind the notion of individual responsibility, on which society insists in the interest of its own survival, and what I have learned about the phenomenon of weariness with life. At such times a single volunteer for death assumes more importance for me than nine hundred and ninety-nine cheerful or complaining bearers of life's burdens.

I myself, I believe, am a burden bearer without illusions, specifically of the complaining type, and I would gladly pass on my load to anyone willing to take it. Why should I of all people be saddled with these outcasts? True, I fell into this trap of my own free will, but at least I feel entitled to gripe about it. I am an underpaid, disabused, middle-level official like hundreds of others; even when I have change in my pocket, I tend to cross the street when I see a beggar; I hate visiting sick people in the hospital; I grumble when I have to stand up for an old lady on the bus; rather than listen to the sniveling of the widower next door, I avoid saying good morning to him. Why, then, have I chosen a job that obliges me, day after day, to put up with the stench of other people's suffering? How could I possibly summon up enough sympathy to contend with the misery that is wearing out the chair on the other side of my desk?

All this complaining makes me feel like a toothless janitor with an inflamed bladder: the doorbell rings in the middle of the night; he pulls a sheepskin coat over his nightshirt, puts a woolen cap on his bald head, and shuffles out—there's no one at the door. He is about to curse the joker when a slight whimper penetrates the cotton-wool plugs in his ears, and looking down he sees a baby wrapped in blankets. The old man can't believe his eyes; he rubs his neck and looks helplessly up and down the deserted street; then—and his reaction could not be more from the heart—he begins to bluster and curse, wishing the depositor of the bundle the worst of all possible futures. For good measure, if he's given to dramatic rhetoric, he will lodge a complaint with Providence: "Why me, O

Lord? There's Pikor at number three and Zahorec at number seven. Why did the bitch have to leave her brat here at number five? Why did she pick me, of all people? Tell me, O Lord, didn't you have something to do with it?" In all likelihood Providence will lie low and say nothing, and the janitor soon wearies of questioning it. Of course, he could put the squalling gift down at Pikor's or Zahorec's door, ring the bell, and scuttle back, but he doesn't. Maybe he's afraid of getting caught, or thinks the baby might catch cold; and maybe, come right down to it, he secretly approves of the unknown person's choice. Pikor is too fond of the bottle, while Zahorec is just getting too soft in the head. As he gathers up the infant, who is wailing violently by now, his mind turns to practical considerations. Later, while washing diapers, he has almost given up wondering why he, number five, rather than someone else, should have been saddled with this none-too-agreeable task.

2

When they no longer have the strength to take the abuse hurled at them from the other end of the line, they smash the window of the locked phone booth of their lives and plunge headlong into the void. Nowadays my clients lack stamina. It is the same kind of weariness that makes prisoners break out of the carelessly guarded camps; the empty cots around them spur their impatience and they leave the Nissen huts for the swirling void beyond the barbed wire.

Not so long ago Mrs. K—— started the parade. Her husband had been beating her for years and she was sick of it. "We'll hale your husband into court," I told her, but she asked me not to. Taking a couple of apples and a camp stool, she rode out to Hüvösvölgy on the streetcar. In her worn-down shoes she stumbled up the hill over the snow-covered rubble. Next day her footprints, like the bullet holes on the whitewashed wall of a peasant cottage, guided the patrolman's eyes to the hilltop. She had eaten her apples, tied a clothesline to an oak that had withered to the shape of a gnarled hand, and kicked away the stool. When they found her, the plastic clothesline had stretched under her weight, so that Mrs. K—— was actually standing. Her false teeth protruded from between her lips, and there was congealed blood on her face where she had clawed herself. In her pocket we found family photographs, which I asked the detective to leave with me for her children. Her husband as a sergeant, sitting in a dragon-headed ship on the merry-go-round. In a retouched color photograph of her wedding, she is hiding her swollen belly under a bunch of Michaelmas daisies. Group pictures bear witness to the passage of time: gurgling babies, behind them brothers and sisters with white socks and set expressions, and at the back the parents, on whose faces a hasty, careless hand seems to have sketched a network of meaningless wrinkles; their lips are sunken, their eyes empty, as though little by little they had lost their power to retain images. Mrs. K—— seems to be saying: "Mother of God, I lead the life of an ox." Her husband didn't like to beat her with his hands; he preferred to kick her, or if he was very drunk, set fire to the hair on her pubis and under her armpits. The children looked on, trembling. K——'s face is dull, its only expression is one of vanity; if someone slapped him, it would make him sad—he might even cry a bit. Somebody told me that after the funeral he propped the dead woman's picture against the wine bottle and stared at it, holding his head in his hands. The next day I took the children away to a home. K—— came to protest; he banged on my desk and shook my typewriter, so I threw him out. A few days ago we met in a bar. Between hiccups he was telling two chimney sweeps how clean his wife had kept everything. His audience turned away, listened to somebody else, and laughed. K—— noticed me and nodded a greeting; he was grimy, had lost weight, and had developed a tic in one eye.

My next client, Mrs. O——, was trying to shake off her obsession with a spyglass. "He makes holes in the ceiling, sticks in the spyglass and peeks at us," she complained of her husband. O—— had left his wife and twin sons for a woman bartender. If he didn't care, I told her, he wouldn't look. "He's only showing that other woman what I've come to, and then they laugh at me," she countered. I encouraged her to arouse her husband's jealousy, to put on a little weight, buy a nice dress, and take a lover. She tried it, took men up to her room, but "she didn't do what she was supposed to," as one of them, a butcher, admitted later. In bed she seemed to be boasting to some third party about her lover's virility; she kept making faces and giggling at the ceiling. From time to time a fit of weeping would come over her and she begged the butcher to hide under the bed with her. He didn't feel like it. Mrs. O——'s occasional lovers stopped coming, even though she had a two-room apartment and her body was still young. "He drives everyone away from me," she complained of her husband. I suggested that she move. She did—several times, in fact. From the fourth floor she moved down to the second, and from there to the ground floor. The apartments got worse and worse, but the spyglass kept breaking through the ceiling right over her bed. Mrs. O——, who had been spying on her husband, projected her pathological curiosity onto him. "They were walking in front of me the day before yesterday. My husband kept pulling at that bitch's ear, but all the while he was making eyes at every woman who passed. He turned to look at one of them, saw me, and started to come over. But I spat at him and ran away . . . Every night he looks through

24

his spyglass and says to his bitch: 'You see, as long as she had me she was alive; I leave her and it nearly kills her. . . .' He's right. Without him I've got nothing. Not even the two children, I never see them any more." She kept threatening to kill herself. I tried mechanically to comfort her. So many people had bandied that threat; more high-sounding phrases had been spoken in this room than on Lear's barren heath. One night she did actually turn on the gas, but left the kitchen door wide open. One of her sons woke up, hauled his mother away from the oven, and opened all the windows. From then on, while one son slept, the other bit his hand to keep awake. Then one night Mrs. O—— mixed some sleeping powder into their supper and tried again. This time the cat woke up, leaped at the door handle, and roused the whole house with its howls. The twins were still alive, but their mother, who had put the rubber gas pipe in her mouth, was done for. Now and then I get a letter from the twins, telling me how they are getting along with their arithmetic or history at school.

In 1951 thirteen-year-old Klara G——'s father was denounced as a war criminal and mass murderer and hanged. G——, the detective in charge of the case, fell in love with her mother, and resigned from the police force so he could marry her. He was expelled from the Party and became a truck driver. The woman also worked, as a nurse. G—— adopted the child, and the three of them lived in harmony. The girl knew only G—— as her father. After 1956 the detective went back to his former employment. Last year the grandmother on the father's side looked the girl up, told her the circumstances of her birth, and tried to stir up some affection for the memory of her real father. This winter, Klara came to me and told me her adoptive father had forced her to have intercourse with him on several occasions; her detailed account seemed credible enough. I asked her whether she knew that, if the accusation proved true, G——would be sent to prison. She nodded. She knew—

25

that's what she wanted. A medical examination showed that she was indeed no longer a virgin. I called in Mrs. G——; at first she protested, then grew uncertain and burst into tears. Searching her memory, she recalled one occasion when, coming home early from night duty at the hospital, she found her husband and daughter together in bed. When she lifted the quilt, she saw that the girl's nightgown had slid up, leaving her naked to the armpits, and that G——'s hand was resting on her belly. She had asked them about it at breakfast, and they had told her that Klara, frightened by the storm the night before, had cuddled up to her father in the parental bed. The mother had also noticed that her husband often went into the bathroom when the girl was washing. And there had been another suspicious incident: some months before, Klara had come into their room just as she and her husband were embracing; she had looked at them, slammed the door, gone into her own room, and locked the door after her. For days after that she had refused to speak to them. Since there were no witnesses, I asked the woman to keep an eye on her husband. Instead of doing so, Mrs. G—— questioned the girl and found the details revoltingly credible. Among other things the girl quoted the terms of endearment used by her foster father during love-making; they sounded very familiar. Mrs. G—— rushed off to her husband's superior and told him the whole story from start to finish. The commanding officer, who disliked G—— to begin with, had dismissed G—— at once and put him under arrest, to prevent him from intimidating his family during the investigation.

A complete report was already in the hands of the public prosecutor when Klara G—— turned up again at my office, informed me that not a word of what she had said was true, and asked me to protect her from her parents' wrath. Why had she done it? I asked. "He sent my real father to the gallows. I wanted him to be interrogated, too, I wanted him to be scared." I remarked that her father by blood had

26

killed defenseless people and been sentenced to death according to law. "His job isn't very appetizing either," she replied. "What about your virginity?" "I tore it myself." When I asked her why she had chosen this particular form of revenge, she said she had often dreamed about it; the idea kept cropping up in her thoughts. Besides, she had noticed that when she sat in G——'s lap his face turned red and his trousers got hard; she'd done it several times just to make sure. What about all the details she had provided? She had spied on them and listened through the keyhole. G—— wasn't let out until a week later. I couldn't prevent the mother from thrashing the child; then one day the stepfather came in and asked me to put Klara in an institution, at least for a while. It was more than he could do to control his bitterness toward the "mass murderer's daughter." Klara wrote nothing for two months, then she sent off long letters asking her stepfather's forgiveness and imploring him to come and see her. G—— did not answer, and his wife wrote instead: "For the moment your father cannot bring himself to forget, so you won't be able to come home this year." Klara G—— picked a deadly amanita in the woods near the institution, broke a razor blade and a pocket mirror into small pieces, then swallowed the whole business. When they found her in the clearing, she was still alive; she died in the ambulance.

B—— was a subdued, retiring sort. For days no one could get a word out of him. Year in, year out, he had lifted two hundred 180-pound sacks of wheat a day, and carried them twenty-five or thirty yards with no more than an occasional break for a cigarette between sacks. After work he drank a pint of beer, except on Saturdays when he had two, but he never touched hard liquor. The roast duck he had on his birthday was well earned. That day he was sitting on the edge of the bed, as usual watching his daughters doing their homework; his shoulders trembled a little, his fists were dangling between his knees. Just as his wife was taking the duck out of the oven, he stood up and went to the kitchen for a smoke. The first puff of smoke or perhaps his fatigue made him reel, and he banged his shin on the open door of the oven. It hurt, then it stopped hurting, then it hurt again; he put up with it for a time, but then the pain was so bad that he went to a doctor. It was cancer of the bone; first they amputated to the knee, three months later to mid-thigh. He was given a crutch and a disablement allowance equal to half of what he had made before. His wife drove herself until she could hardly stand, packing noodles into paper bags on a conveyor belt, but even so she was unable to earn more than twelve hundred forints a month. The girls grew out of their clothes, there was no money for Christmas presents, they gave up meat. It was only then that they realized how small the apartment was. A cupboard, two beds, a table, and two chairs were crowded into a space fifteen feet square. This left little room to move around in, so that B——, unable to make much use of his crutch, would hop around on one leg, taking care not to bump his aching, occasionally suppurating stump. When the doctor learned that B—— slept in the same bed as his wife, he called her in and made her promise to sleep somewhere else, because she might kick her husband's injured leg in her sleep and the slightest blow could be dangerous—he almost said fatal. Mrs. B—— moved to the floor—there was a space about eighteen inches wide between the cupboard and the bed. They spread out some old coats, and there she lay, tossing and moaning. Sleepless, her husband propped himself up in bed and looked at his wife as the moonlight shone upon her worn face. One night he pleaded with her to sleep beside him; Mrs. B——, almost angrily, refused. Her husband snapped at her: "I suppose I disgust you." She was offended and didn't say a word to him for a whole day. In the meantime I got after the housing department. "Possibly next year, but most likely in eighteen months or more," said my exhausted colleague, sucking

28

furiously at his pipe. For B—— those were agonizing days. Washing was difficult, and he couldn't hop to the toilet by himself; he needed help. His daughters spoke to him less and less, stopped asking how he was feeling, and aired the place out more often than ever before. He and his wife had nothing to say to each other either; she complained about her job, but he didn't even have that much to talk about. If he had any pleasure in life, it was eating. Mrs. B—— once remarked, jokingly perhaps: "You eat more than when you used to carry sacks." Her husband brooded over this for days, and came to the conclusion that he really had grown fat—from potatoes and beans. Every morning he chatted with a blind man who lived in the house. In the course of these chats he would reckon out loud how much more his food and tobacco cost than the amount the family would lose if the postman delivered a widow's pension each month instead of his disability allowance. The blind man, who didn't understand what he was getting at, agreed with him. "Yes," he said, "life is expensive." One morning B—— polished off a bottle of lye, and for good measure a glassful of nicotine. Not wanting to soil the bed, he sat down on the stone floor of the kitchen to die and tied a handkerchief around his mouth to prevent his death rattle from being heard in the hallway outside. His last utterance was characteristically laconic. On a page torn from a school copybook he wrote: "Sell my best suit to pay for the funeral."

3

This afternoon I shall probably have to go out, to take an idiot child to a home. His parents—Dr. Endre Bandula and his wife, née Borbála Cséfalvay—poisoned themselves the day before yesterday. They were lying under a rumpled down quilt on a bed supported by bricks, with only rags between them and the bare springs. On their bedside table lay the Tibetan Book of the Dead, some lottery tickets, and a large piece of bacon rind. Their five-year-old lay naked and hairy on a bed slimy with excrement.

The neighbors broke down the door twelve hours after the parents had died. Bandula and his wife despised their neighbors but did not hesitate to sponge on them; the neighbors on the other hand felt sorry for the Bandulas but were always denouncing them to the authorities. I myself received six such complaints, but there was nothing I could do about them. Bandula clowned, flattered me, lost his temper, and occasionally tried to frighten me with simulated fainting spells. But his basic attitude toward me was one of indifference; his certificate attesting to a stay in a mental hospital made him invulnerable—a plain-clothesman's badge or a leper's sores could not have been more effective. Mrs. Bandula would talk in a dying voice about her happy childhood and her unusual religion; she would complain of her deceased stepmother's severity and the spitefulness of the neighbors. Now and then she would drop a word about the family's straitened circumstances, but if I brought up the subject of the child she answered evasively and fell silent. Now and then she would raise her tired eyes to mine; for a moment her unabashed humility paralyzed me, then both of us would look at the typewriter. Her whole body sagged—cheeks, nose, breasts, belly, even her arms. One by one her teeth vanished, first the natural ones, then the gold crowns; she lisped slightly and kept licking her discolored but still fleshy lips. I'm told she was beautiful once, but all she cared about now was eating: the proceeds from the Chinese fans and crested bone china they took to rummage sales, the various allowances provided by relatives, church, and state—all went into food for Mrs. Bandula and drink for her husband; the child got the short end of it. Still, it was he who survived. Right now he's standing on his bed, rubbing his indestructible fuzzy body against the wooden bars of his cot, playing with his genitals and chortling. The other tenants will feed him for a day or two, but no longer. I ought to take him to a home, but there's no room for him anywhere. For the moment I have no idea what to do with Ferike Bandula; I'm afraid I'll be stuck with him. His ribs stick out and he likes having them tickled; it makes him scream with superhuman happiness. Every time I go near him, I give him a tickle.

During the war Bandula, who had a degree in law and political science, was a ministerial assistant and the owner of a four-story apartment house. He himself lived in a three-room apartment on the third floor with his mother and wife. His only concession to the right-wing tendency of the day was that as a landlord he evicted a Jewish fishmonger and a typist with a dislocated hip who was suspected of Communist sympathies, but he secretly made it up to them with money and another apartment. At the office he steered clear of politics, and whenever statistics seemed unduly alarming, he would tuck them away in more reassuring categories. He liked his work, and kept quiet when his colleagues disparaged the moral and technical preparedness of the Allied powers. He deliberately arranged to make a rather simple-minded impression, and showed such modesty in presenting his reports to his busy superiors that they were only too pleased to promote him. His colleagues confided in him— their private opinions and the ups and downs of their marital irregularities. Bandula would nod and smile with an air of knowing sympathy.

When he came home at night, he would go first to his mother's room—as long as she lived. He would kiss her hand and tell her about his day at the ministry, embroidering a bit to amuse her. Not until this rite was disposed of could he go to his wife. The old woman was a light sleeper, and when she heard their bed creaking at night, she would come hobbling into the young couple's room and bang the quilt with her stick, saying: "That's enough for tonight,

Endre, I beg you! You've got a day's work ahead of you at the office. Is that clear?" "Yes, Mother," came the voice from the dark. "And you, Piroska. I haven't heard you say anything." His wife, whose name was Borbála, always surrendered: "Yes, Mother." Somewhat mollified, the old woman wished them good night, and tapping the chair and table legs with her stick, groped her way back to her canopy-surmounted bed with its never-extinguished lamp. Then she would spend the rest of the night looking at herself in the mirror.

A little girl was born to them. Bandula barked on all fours to make her laugh, while his wife pressed the child to her spreading naked body every morning, and for a year and a half they talked of nothing else but the baby and everything it did. During the siege the grandmother took her up to the yard for air, and a low-flying fighter gunned them both down. Bandula's howling was a torment to the other occupants of the air-raid shelter; his wife, who was half out of her senses, cradled the child's body in her arms and refused to let it be buried; eventually it was taken from her while she was asleep. On that day Bandula began to let his reddish beard grow, and for months after his wife would wear no dress but the one she had had on when holding her child for the last time. With the little girl gone, they had nothing more to say to each other; both spent their days staring into space and let their apartment and possessions go to rack and ruin. From then on they lived without hope from day to day.

After the war the bearded Bandula was dismissed because he had served under the former regime. Their house was nationalized, other tenants were moved into two of their rooms, and later one of there, who had a second cousin working in the housing department, successfully claimed exclusive rights to the bathroom. Bandula appealed, whereupon the other tenant, a former Fascist dentist, denounced him to the police for hoarding jewelry and spreading alarmist rumors he picked up on foreign radio stations. Bandula was interned for a year, and his mother's rings and brooches were confiscated. One of the guards in the camp took a great delight in tormenting him: he would offer him a chair, slap him for his insolence if he sat down, and slap him for disobeying an order if he remained standing. Bandula returned home with his mind unhinged.

Before his arrest he had had a job as a hod carrier; afterward he didn't want to work. He sat huddled in their cluttered room, looking out the window, which was kept closed even in fine weather, at the uninspired comings and goings on the market square below; he was afraid to go out, and when he had to he always carried a medical certificate testifying to his schizophrenia in his wallet. When they had sold everything they could, he looked for work. He was hired several times, but when reprimanded for his idle daydreaming, he regularly panicked and asked for his papers. In the end he abandoned all thought of regular employment and took to writing poems about his daughter's death. His wife would type them in several copies, and tricked out with green spectacles and a white cane, he would peddle them in cafés and snack bars. He wouldn't say a word, but would merely hold a sheaf of poems under a prospective customer's nose, at the same time producing a card with the words: "Help a poor disabled veteran. His own poems for only one forint." Some gave him two forints, but most gave him nothing.

This occupation appealed to him, and he ranged over the whole city. Behind his green spectacles he would recapitulate his bleak existence, and when the spirit moved him he would spend his easy earnings on drink. What drew him to liquor was more the effect than the taste; if he could get good and drunk, everything was fine, it didn't matter in the least whether he was a ministerial assistant or a beggar. In either case, whether sitting in a red velvet armchair fragrant with cigar smoke or on top of a sour-smelling wine barrel, he was a spectator, watching his fellow human beings—and in either case his fellow human beings were unpredictable and terrifying.

He began to get drunk in the mornings, and would upset tables as he lurched through the cafés with his poems. The waitresses got sick of him and put him out, and sometimes—despite his medical certificate—a policeman would slap his face in a nearby doorway. One policeman kicked him on the knee; the ache died down but never left him entirely. It amused him to limp; at first he exaggerated his limp only slightly, then he began to drag his leg much more than necessary. Sometimes he and his wife were close to starvation, and then he would try to cut down on his drinking. He would skulk around bars; when one of the drinkers had gone to the men's room, Bandula would cautiously drink what was left in his glass and make himself scarce. Sometimes he was caught in the street: when he heard the clatter of feet behind him, he knew what to expect and burst into tears. He would put up his right hand to protect his neck and his left hand to cover his face, and burst into a shrill whine. His attackers expected him to protest his innocence, or abuse them, or run away. His groveling disconcerted them, and after punching him once or twice for the sake of form, they would agree that "the old man's off his rocker," and send him on his way. Once in a while they even called him back and treated him to a drink.

Mrs. Bandula learned shorthand and typing and found a job. And something else happened in her life: she joined a newly founded religious sect, the Society of the Penitent God. It gave her great satisfaction to know that the society had only two hundred members in this world and that they all knew one another. Their leader was a gaunt man with a goiter and a perpetual sweat who lived with his three children and harmonium in the back room of an old lady's shop and worked as an assistant in the autopsy room of a cancer hospital. His faithful often came to see him in his place of work; and there—amid the man-sized refrigerator pans, the chopped bodies and flayed limbs—they found it easier to understand the extraordinary commandments of their new faith.

"Live as if you were going to die before morning," he preached. He never used the word "forbidden"; his pet word was "unnecessary," and as he said it, his hand in its bloodstained rubber glove would scythe the air with special emphasis. His followers usually met in subcells of four or five; they reminded one another of the futility of everything that others were so bent on acquiring that they wore themselves out and tormented their fellow men in the process. The governing principle of life, they said, is God's suffering, and men are drops of the divine sweat. In our death, He does penance for the patent imperfection of Creation; our reward beyond this life—His well-earned triumph—is the glittering void, a beatific formlessness, perfect repose, and silence. To appease God's suffering, they said, we must try, even in our present life, to free ourselves from the muck, from everything that is oppressive, violent, and perishable, and from every stirring of human pride. The members of the assembly despised politics, avoided the printed word, went about in hideous though comfortable rags, sang a good deal, made love to each other as the fancy struck them, and though attaching no great importance to food, ate quite a lot.

Mrs. Bandula, the daughter of a former provincial notable, daydreamed at her work, which she did very slowly. Not infrequently her attention flew off while her boss was dictating to her, and by the time she returned to dull reality she had omitted whole paragraphs. The stockings on her thickset legs were riddled with runs, and her sweater had a tendency to bunch up at the sides, baring patches of sallow, pasty skin. At political meetings she munched peanuts and often kept her seat when everyone else stood up to cheer. When taken to task, she admitted with a smile that she hadn't been listening. If her presence was nevertheless tolerated for several years, it was thanks to her boss, whose private assignments she typed at a ridiculously low rate in the afternoon, when everyone else had gone home. Once he pressed her to tell him why she was so listless. She saw no reason not to tell him about the main events of her life and the religious sect she belonged to. Her boss was amused; after observing that her religion sounded perfectly reasonable to him, he asked her whether the worshipers of the Penitent God were bound to abstinence. Not at all, she said. And did their religion authorize sexual pleasure? She replied in the affirmative, offered no resistance as he led her to the work table in the darkened office, panted without restraint, and while putting her clothes in order made no reference to what had happened. She never asked if they might meet under other circumstances, caressed the man's sinewy body with absent-minded gentleness, and encouraged him by muttering obscene words. But one day, when at the end of a page the man suddenly seized her and without a word dragged her to the short, hard table, Mrs. Bandula began to cry and shouted angrily that from then on she wouldn't type a single line outside of office hours. Whereupon her boss withdrew his protection and Mrs. Bandula was dismissed.

Two years later, after an unwanted pregnancy, the Bandulas' male child was born. Backache, pains in the heart area, and edematous swellings warned them that their second child would be a child of tribulation. Prior to its advent, the couple were living in extreme poverty, subsisting on a meager allowance sent them by relatives in America. A Caesarean was needed, and for long minutes afterward the baby refused to cry; as they feverishly restored it to life, Mrs. Bandula's ample body sprawled in a swoon on the blood-splattered operating table. When she first nursed the infant, the mother noticed that the rhomboid fontanel was missing from the child's skull. The explanation given her at the hospital was terse: the seams of the bone segments had knitted together in the womb. In the first few weeks of its life the Bandulas took the child from one hospital to another, but the doctors avoided the eyes of the desperate, humiliated parents. Finally, an old doctor looked them in the face and said: "I regret to say that the child will be an idiot. There's nothing we can do." The Bandulas did not understand. "It will be able to eat, walk, and perhaps use a chamber pot, but not much else." He asked them if they wanted to bring it up—or, to be more precise, train it—themselves. If they applied at once, he said, they could send it to a home for retarded children in a year or two. Utterly dismayed, the parents declined to do so.

The couple took the child to their slatternly hearts, but did no more for it than they did for themselves. On second thought, I should say, probably less. True, they kept it, and made no attempt to liberate themselves by finding it a place in a home. But their sacrifice brought them only ridicule; some doubted their good faith and others were repelled by the motives—at once instinctive and perverse—of their decision.

For all his parents' efforts, the child could not learn to use the pot. When he was three, his skin became allergic to rubber pants. His thighs became inflamed, but without the pants his clothes got wet, which resulted in sore throats, pleurisy, and endless bladder trouble; he was constantly coughing, spitting, and vomiting. After vainly consulting any number of doctors in an attempt to escape the vicious circle of rubber pants and chills, the Bandulas decided to raise the child as a savage. It would either harden him or kill him. At the height of summer they stripped him naked, and when autumn came they did not put his clothes back on again. They bought no firewood, lest the changes in temperature prevent him from adapting

37

to the cold. They eliminated cooked food from his diet and gave him carrots, onions, and black radishes to munch all day, with an occasional portion of raw horsemeat, liver, and brains. Feri grew stronger, his colds vanished, and a thick blond down spread over his whole body.

The other tenants and the neighbors suspected the parents, especially Bandula himself, the inventor of the cure, of wanting to murder their child. They reported their suspicions to every conceivable government office, declaring that the former owner of the house ought to be in jail, while the unfortunate child would be better off in a home. Their wordy depositions converged in my office, and after due investigation ended up in the filing department. And because of my inaction I was accused of aiding and abetting attempted murder disguised as a toughening-up cure. I did indeed leave the Bandulas in peace. From time to time I summoned them to my office; we talked, they signed a meaningless statement to the effect that they had been duly warned, and everything went on as before. Life has an intrinsic value, I philosophized; no one is justified, on any grounds whatever, in disposing of a human life, however ill favored; but as I said this I was haunted by the memory of certain institutions, where fermenting lumps of flesh lie in baskets or cribs, breathing but giving no other sign of life, living because there is no one to murder them. Nor should there be, I said to myself patiently and stupidly. When the first denunciation came in, I went to see the Bandulas myself.

Feri was stamping about in his crib on an excrement-stained nylon sheet strewn with apple cores, cabbage stalks, carrot ends, a bare rib of mutton, and various unidentifiable scraps of meat. It was the same carpet of miscellaneous garbage as in the monkey house at the zoo. In a paroxysm of happiness the child rattled the bars of his crib, rubbed his muscular stomach up against them, and greeted me with a screech. His eyes were full of a consuming expectancy. Besides the child, I found only Bandula at home. Clad in a black raincoat, he was lying on the bare bedsprings. He had a light blue towel around his neck, and there were bread crumbs and ashes in his beard. He was holding a tattered crime novel entitled *The Fakir's Revenge;* the cover showed a shaggy head sticking out of the ground. I looked around. On the table stood an uncovered saucepan containing a three-day supply of noodles, a fan, a pair of underdrawers, some obsolete bank notes, bread crusts, pumpkin seeds, a mouth organ, and an alarm clock without a dial; on the chair a chamber pot, the remains of a candle, and a paper lantern. A black lace brassière hung from the window fastening; in a corner two stringless tennis racquets, on a shelf an alcohol stove, an illustrated horoscope, some old lottery tickets with a rubber band around them, and a cheese bell with two white mice inside. The burlap and brown paper that replaced the broken window panes admitted a murky light. The wall was peeling with damp; on it I noticed a few blood spots, and above the child's bed some brownish streaks the width of a fingertip. I had no desire to sit down, but after a while lowered myself on to a rickety kitchen chair strewn with damp sugar that stuck to my trousers. The stench in the room was harsh, intense, unbearable.

"Humble greetings, Comrade," said Bandula, propping himself up with his elbow. His eyes described rapid, frightened circles around me. Tugging at his beard, he asked if I had come from the police. In that case there was more room outside, unless of course I had a search warrant. His circumstances weren't exactly a bed of roses, but he didn't have to put up with illegal persecution. Before I had time to reassure him, he became frightened at his own words and took refuge in his infirmity, pulling up his trouser leg, fingering his calf, and to make his situation perfectly clear, producing his discharge from the mental hospital. Then, in a new access of aggressiveness, he demanded to know what decision the authorities had come to in his case, because rather than be led away to prison he would jump out the window. When he finally understood that I had not come from the police, he stretched out comfortably, asked for a cigarette, and said he was ready to discuss anything, from the state of the weather to Roman law.

In the hour and a half I spent with him he poured forth a mixture of platitudes, incomprehensible allusions, idiotic lies, and astonishing truths; he boasted and cringed, cursed and whined by turns. From time to time he would jump up, take a spoonful of the cold, greasy noodles, kiss his son, or sweep the litter off his sheet. With increasing assurance he kept asking for cigarettes. "As the holder of a degree in law," he resolutely insisted that the child's life was his business, although he knew he was risking arrest by his attitude. He and his wife, he pointed out, fed the boy and kept him clean without help from anyone. The child had been living with them for thirteen hundred days, and in all that time they had not been free from worry over him for a single day or been able to share their worries with anyone. Accordingly, all he asked was to be left alone. There was so much misery in the world, so many objects of pity, why should people bother about them? And anyone who disagreed could go to hell. I should realize, he said, that nobody could hurt him; he had nothing to lose except—here he waved at his surroundings—this. He would be as free in prison as he was here on his bedspring with his son. "One time in the madhouse I felt like singing. I sang the first tune that entered my head. The orderly came over, tied my hands behind my back, and attached them to the radiator. I asked him why. It hurt. He said, 'So you'll rot.' I said, 'I'm human, too, why should I rot?' 'You human?' he said, and spat. He went away, leaving me tied there, but I could see he was thinking. After a while he came back and said: 'What

40

if you are human? You can rot anyway. Look around, see how many human beings there are right here in this small room.' All the same, he untied me and we played cards. Look, my dear colleague, we've both learned the same Roman law. Remember all those principles, rules, and punishments? If I may say so, you're still a slave to all that. You rarely think of yourself—only, let's say, when you have a toothache. None of that applies to me. Not a single human word applies to me. I'm no more human than my son. Let's have a cigarette. I'm a freak. Of course, that, too, is a human word." We both laughed. He peeled a carrot for his son, we watched him munch it, and then I left.

That was the beginning of our acquaintance. He at once appealed to me and repelled me. The naked hollows of his being reminded me of my foreclosed opportunities. I even dreamed about him: handcuffed, he led me along a barred-off corridor where, at regular intervals, jackbooted guards brooded outside gray, felt-padded doors. In another dream he was sitting bolt upright at my desk, his long fingers resting on the keys of my typewriter; he warned me that I must tell the truth, and started a file on my case. After noting my name, date, and place of birth, etc., he asked me whether I liked and respected him. I replied that I was not at all sure. He shoved aside the typewriter and bellowed in my face: "Admit you want my job! You envy me my responsibility! Is this what you want?" And he held out his right leg, to which a ball and chain were attached.

Finally, the neighbors denounced Bandula to his parcel-sending American relatives. This time their efforts were successful. They wrote that he treated his child like an animal, sold the parcels, and drank up the money, that their assistance only encouraged his laziness. "I don't know what we'd eat if our relatives didn't help us," Mrs. Bandula once said. She was no longer capable of office work, and her heart condition prevented her from doing anything more strenuous. Every two months she would quit her job in the hope of finding something less fatiguing and better paid, but eventually she abandoned the whole idea and went out as a cleaning woman. At first she got work every day; then she ceased to be in demand and took to her bed. They needn't have starved, since I arranged for them to get free lunches. They had only to save some of the food and there would have been enough for supper. The manager of the soup kitchen complained that half the time they didn't even come to pick up their lunch.

As a final resort I tried to get Bandula a job. The removal of corpses interested him, and he asked me to put in a word for him at a hospital. This kind of work, he explained, required a sense of dignity and a severe, enigmatic facial expression. Just the thing for him, he felt. In one of the hospitals he followed a young corpse bearer around, an impudent young fellow: dance music blared from the transistor that he kept in the pocket of his white coat; in addition, he was a wag. One of his tricks was to slip an old woman under a shroud face down on top of an old man lying on his back.

Bandula declared that he would treat the dead with the respect they deserved. Eventually he got the job he wanted, had his white coat dyed black, and sewed a yellow memento mori on the back of it. His outfit was not appreciated by his superiors. Later he borrowed a portable record player, and dug up a record of Beethoven's funeral march; from then on the solemn strains swelled up from the depths of his rubber-tired trolley. The difficulty was that he was unable to lift the corpses, and had to ask such patients as could walk to lend him a helping hand. He propelled his vehicle rather recklessly, and on one occasion spilled his load in front of an expectant mother. He didn't last a week. I was very sorry. If he had not been so demanding at the start, if he had been willing to learn the trade from watching others, they might have come to tolerate his unusual personality in what was after all an unusual job. A little money, a regular routine, the pride in work well done—sometimes nothing more is needed to keep a man going.

Those people were a thorn in my side, but now that they've killed themselves, I have to admit that no one will rub the woolly back of their idiot child as good-naturedly as they did. I'm a busy man, and their visits were definitely a nuisance, but I'd be glad to see them coming through the door right now. They had their place in the world, even if it was no bigger than the bullet holes in the roughcast of our houses.

4

Those who die by their own hands deserve our respect. Actors whom no one has hired, they give the best of themselves before God and the neighbors. They throw us out of their balloons like so much ballast, and from our moldering walls we watch them—the pioneers—as they pass through the golden gates to nothingness.

The long procession twines itself toward the crematory. Those who fall out of line are struck down. Those who are defeated, whose eyes look beyond the world of men, who have cast off our sufferings, who have chosen the void for a mother, the abyss for a father, and clods of earth for brothers and sisters, who have ceased to savor the delirious sweetness of the moment to come, who have learned to disobey the trembling of their knees and the chattering of their teeth, who are able to slip out of their bodies as easily as a snake from its skin—shall we call them madmen? cowards? malingerers? Shall I drag them back by the hair, shall I press them to linger one more minute, one more day, just a little longer? No, dear Lord, that would be asking too much of me; I stay in line and keep step with the best of them. The most I can do is ask you, if it depends on you, not to take any more of my clients away. Let them bear their cross down here with me; they're used to it, I'm used to it, let them go on bearing it . . . as usual.

TOPOGRAPHY

I go from door to door in this part of town, this gray-brown realm of unrelieved weariness, this past that is merely a grimy present, these streets that are neither modern nor old-fashioned—even in their prime they must have been ugly and decay must have set in before the newness had worn off—this dispirited frown on the face of the city. Idling awhile in the angles of their shrunken geometry, I itemize the plexus of cracks, the mold, the soot, the crimson blotches of rust, the pockmarks left by bullets, the patches of bastard replastering, the even coat of grime on the walls. What was once smooth and sturdy is crumbling away, what was ingeniously functional sticks out, naked and ashen. Stone, timber, and iron are jumbled as haphazardly as chicken giblets on a platter. Discolored name plates, walled-up windows, shattered blinds, mutilated lions'-heads, eternally splotched and splattered doorways, urine-stained rosettes, sagging gutters and cables, eviscerated sirens, tumbledown fences with grotesque fleur-de-lys-headed spikes, ponderous padlocks guarding orphaned basements, abandoned brooms, mildewed piles of bicycle chains and cardboard trumpets, concrete boils marking the entrances of air-raid shelters, shot-up windows loosely fixed with bricks, obsolete posters—I like these houses. Three or four generations have worn themselves out in them, impregnating them with the smell of vanished seasons and happenings. Dinosaurs of the first industrial revolution, they have fallen out of history. Their door handles were made to preserve the fingerprints of people without importance, and now, in their disciplined death agony, their only dialogue is with the wind, the rain, and the frost.

As I walk along these overripe façades, the ditches slow me down, forcing me to move in uncertain leaps. Fatigue settles in the cracks in the roadway; I find it more and more difficult to lift my feet. Here and there the drowsy neighborhood comes to life. The street I am entering now was once the heart of the red-light district; the saloons, brothels, and shady hotels are gone, replaced by lodging houses into which the nearby railroad station disgorges homeless provincials, job-hunting peasants, wrathful families in pursuit of runaway fathers, and innumerable children, who move too fast for my attention to keep pace. On the creaking, shored-up spiral stairway I step over a slumbering old man. In the apartments galoshes grow beards of mold, cockroaches scurry along the cracks in the floorboards, the sheets—when there are any—are stained with bedbug-drawn blood. The people who live here have given up hope of lying comfortably in bed, of stretching out or making love in peace; the plaster flakes off on them, the drains leak on their necks, rats gnaw the baby's toes, the sick urinate on the healthy. To be shut up with a demented father, a mother-in-law with cancer of the rectum, or a husband who keeps a cleaver under his pillow calls for stern self-discipline. An old woman gets an electric shock, an invalid falls out of the window, police sirens scream, and then it's a working day again. One of the lodgers has gonorrhea, another plays the trumpet, the third sits for hours in the communal toilet, the fourth collects stray cats or rags, or dry crusts or bones for glue or broken glass or rancid butter, the fifth is a voyeur, the sixth a police informer, the seventh explains the Gospels, the eighth throws knives, the ninth exhibits his boils, and the tenth cadges a bowl of soup, but the eleventh washes the paralytic old woman and helps her drink her milk. The twelfth sits in the doorway and blows soap bubbles for the children, the thirteenth makes fireman's outfits with brass buttons for raffia dolls, the fourteenth agrees with everyone, the fifteenth brings the dying man stewed pears and tells him jokes, the sixteenth lets prurient adolescents into her bed in return for a few buckets of coal, the seventeenth climbs up on the roof to catch an escaped parrot, the eighteenth feeds the neighbor's baby, the nineteenth tells the paralytic girl's fortune and predicts a husband with a car, the twentieth always says hello first, even to the feebleminded.

In fine weather, life overflows into the street: chickens are plucked, fish cleaned, cards and tag played, diapers mended; zither strings and spark plugs bake and cane chairs creak in the sun, golden icons sway on the wall of the urinal, senile old women emerge from the molluscan mullings and propping their elbows on the windowsills peer out at the world, a breeze wafts a free whiff of meat and garlic through the window. At night, big-bosomed girls press tumescent youths to the wall, and from time to time the white summer jacket of a bicycle patrolman passes slowly by. After Epiphany a shivering line forms outside the coal cellar, shaggy old men take their places in unpainted coffins, floorboards are ripped up for firewood, drunkards' pockets are picked as they lie in the snow, double-bass players hobble past on their way to wedding feasts, cats crunch chicken bones, children hide their bare bottoms in harlequins' beds, a bedraggled carnival float passes, and the air rings with the songs of whores and pickpockets newly converted into washroom attendants and night watchmen. It's a wild, hysterical street; some years ago, when I first came here, the people turned away and no one spoke to me. The women were taking wreaths to the unmarked, two-day-old grave of eighteen boys and a girl.

2

Though the house has only two floors, I'm hopelessly lost. I stagger up a perilously steep staircase, grope my way along a soft, sanded corridor and bump into someone. He asks me what time it is. A swinging door, a plank walk, an iron staircase, and I'm down in the unpaved yard. A water faucet in the middle, a toilet in one corner. The splintering door reaches only to waist height; the face of a young girl leans out, below the forehead a smooth band of skin, she has no eyes. "Did you get the sugar?" she asks with an effort. "Yes." I give her some. "You can touch my face," she says gratefully. "Has your mother's new baby arrived?" "He's dead." Smothered under the quilt. Their room measures forty-seven square feet. All three of them sleep in one bed. I've come too late. From the swinging door I look back; the eyeless girl is striking two empty cans together close to her ear.

An iron folding door daubed with gray, hideously gnarled wooden steps; the formerly glassed inner door has been mended with rags and newspaper. Inside, a one-legged man is sitting in the dark, weeping. I take his grandchild away with me.

A light-blue blind on a shop, silence within. I raise the blind. Behind it an iron-framed swinging door. Behind the peephole an unmoving eye, a lashless lid. "Come in." A face ravaged by vitriol. "I know why you're here—I've been expecting you."

A sheet of tar paper is nailed over the door. I roll it up, this looks like sticky business and I don't want my retreat cut off. A meat-colored sailcloth curtain but no stairs; I have to jump. Two men in leather jackets look at me, and go on with their game of chess. A naked young girl is asleep on the bed. I wake her up. "Come on." The two of them step right behind me. "I'll take you home," I tell the girl quietly. I'm careful not to look around.

Spiral stairs down to the laundry room. I make my way through the steam and the dripping sheets. In one corner an ancient crone is sitting on a chamber pot, moaning, grimacing, and stinking—that's how I always find her. A crow is strolling about on the stove; a little boy is feeding it chicken innards. I put money on the table, the old woman grabs at it. The child throws a spoon at her and shows me his school report. A's all the way. "Can I stay with Grandma?" "Yes, you can stay."

The hall leads to the toilet, which opens out on an air-shaft. A kerosene lantern lights up two chests, one of them containing linen. There is a crucifix on the pillow. On the other chest a girl is sitting filing her nails. "Tell me how it happened." "Radish will scratch my eyes out if I tell." I turn up the wick of the lantern. "I'll tell him not to." The girl picks up a bottle of nail polish. "When Radish says he'll do something, he does it."

In the first courtyard a pawnbroker, a chiropodist, and

a palmist. In the second courtyard a blind man weaves baskets, clothes are rented, and waffles are made. In the innermost court a single tall shop window, mirrors with carved gilt frames, the picture of a bride, military medallions, and bicycle handlebars. As I open the door, a clockwork parrot says: "Hurry up, time is money." The picture framer has had a heart attack. He is lying on his back; an automatic steel arm puts a cigar stub in his mouth. A cot with chubby twins romping in it flies up to the ceiling. A rocking chair with the maniacal chief engineer in it, the frame maker's brother, descends from on high. He has ropes and wires in his lap. A woman comes out of the disappearing kitchen with a potful of bean stew. "You live like this and you want to adopt a child?" I ask. The engineer is furious. "Why not? Don't you like our place? I say that space is no problem. A few pulleys, winches, ropes, and the third dimension is mine." I sit down in the rocking chair, set the machinery in motion, and up go the twins. I reject the engineer's application. The woman goes back to her disappearing kitchen, the steel arm with the cigar stub stops moving.

I grope my way through a long basement corridor. Something soft under my foot. A cat? no, a rat; it screams like a child. Somebody clamors from the end of the corridor. I pound on the door and shout who I am. "Break down the door, they've locked me in—the baby's coming." I pull at the handle, it comes away in my hand. I brace my shoulder against the door; nothing happens. I kick a hole in the panel and crawl in. Two yellow feet on the table, behind them on the bed a huge belly arching between them. The peaked head of a child slips out; I press the purple veins on the woman's belly, and already the little body is in my hand, white with amniotic fluid. I press the dripping infant to my chest. It's all there, it's a boy, he squawks like a duck. The mother has fainted, and it's cold. I cover her up, wrap the child in my coat, bundle

50

some rags around its head, and rush upstairs. There's a hairdresser's across the way. They wash it under the faucet, put it under a hair dryer, and wrap it in a woolen shawl. Women in hair curlers run screeching down to the mother. The siren of an ambulance wails; somebody washes the stains off my suit. I feel out of place and make my escape.

3

I arrive at the marketplace. In the center stands a fortresslike red brick building. The small, dust-covered turrets at the corners are supported by brown Atlases. Sky-blue plaster loincloths conceal the private parts of these squat giants, who seem to smile under their burden. Plump pigeons are preening themselves in the nooks and crannies of the brick façade. Down below shopkeepers are gesticulating in their doorways. Along my way, sausages splutter in frying pans, cheeses display their functional sculpture, suspended rabbits swing to and fro, and catfish yawn in glass tanks. Pigs' kidneys, strips of tripe and pigs' feet are laid out in aluminum trays; shops are cluttered with crates of apples, tubs of sauerkraut, and sacks of onions. It takes me several minutes to escape from the magic attraction of rugs with rhymed inscriptions, brass-and-tinsel rings, potato peelers, wonder glues, string ties, china deer, gingerbread hearts, trick cigarettes, obscene wooden dolls, and magnetic mouse traps. Customers are still drifting about, though the foreheads of the plaster giants are already darkening in the twilight, and the market will soon be packing up. The hyacinths get a last watering, the fish are fed a beetle or two, the geese are stowed away in the icebox. The sausages make a last splutter in the pan, the mottled pumpkins are put back into their sacks, and a jet of water rinses the blood from leather aprons and marble slabs. The crash helmet, the corn cutter, and the nutcracker won't be sold until tomorrow. A birch-twig broom raises a whirl of dust, iron gates crash to, metal chairs are folded up, electric switches are shut off. A stall keeper bellows as a mechanical street-sweeper crashes into his display of feather dusters, but the sweeper with its revolving yellow light clatters on, describing a slow rectangle around the stall keeper as he appraises the damage. Two mounted policemen with brick-colored faces arrive in the marketplace, and a corridor of stony glances opens up before them. On one side, the truculent street sweeper lurches and cavorts like a clown; on the other, the two geldings raise their legs above the gun holsters and shit with leaden dignity. And all around the square, the neon beacons of conciliation light up over the movie house, shops, restaurants, and bars.

Under the canopy of vapor lights, late shopping baskets, battered dinner pails, torn leatherette bags pass by. Homecomers are sucked forehead first into gateways; their coats covered with dust, husband and wife flounder homeward as though trudging over sand dunes. The activities of the square impose an itinerary that is difficult to vary. By day the movement is regular and unswerving, but now in the twilight it is enlivened by irrational currents and eddies. On the sidewalk I am sometimes inclined to think that I can go wherever I please, cut across here, turn in there, or loop eccentrically around the block; but I fight off this paranoid temptation and submit to the regulations that confine me to the common stream. The street commands the pedestrian, the doorway the incomer, the stairway the upgoer, the table and chair, glass and knife the homecomer. And if, somewhere in this conveyor belt of obedience, there is a breakdown and the body digresses from the appropriate order of things, the policeman is there—and so am I—to put it right with a few swift and well-tried stratagems.

There is a time to be born and a time to die. A drop
of blood has dried on my hand; in my palm I hold the
memory of a newborn child's fist. In due time, this tender
fist will do everything that needs doing: it will tear, it
will open, it will snatch and strike. It will obey not only
its own time, but also the time of the things it lives with.
Everything it clutches, caresses, or rejects is crystallized
time. Thrusting the days behind him, the child will feed,
wash, and cover himself with the lives of others. He
will pay for everything with time, two weeks for a bed,
an hour for a piece of meat. In so doing, he will accumulate
years. Floor, armchair, and picture frame, inasmuch as
they are trodden on, sat upon, or dusted, will bear witness
to his life. He will drain some people of their substance,
others will suck him dry, and in the end he will be con-
sumed. Possibly the road that will take him to the pit will
be more roundabout than that taken by his parents, but
he will get there just the same.

A number of my clients have smashed up their homes
when drunk. They hurled fragile objects at the wall and
slashed the furniture. Some kicked and spat on the debris,
others merely lit a cigarette and gazed tenderly at the
wreckage as if it were a sleeping child. They had pride,
and were sorry for themselves: all this meaningless profu-
sion into which they had poured their blood left them no
room to move. If that was all the laborious years left
behind, then away with it. But next day they would start
all over again, repairing what could be repaired, and
what was beyond repair they would replace in five or
ten years' time, with a new, better version, just as nations
do after a war. I never took these home breakers' outbursts
very seriously, since their daily routine remained un-
changed. It is easy to kick a wardrobe mirror to pieces,

but what will my client do in the evening? Look, it's already getting dark, but nothing has happened all day. He could have given vent to his spleen on his birthday or wedding anniversary, but he takes it out on the wardrobe. But though his furniture and apartment, his house and street measure out his steps, determine his habits, and trace the map of his relationships, though they bring him gnawing little humiliations, offend him with their ugliness, arouse his lust for vengeance, set him against his loved ones, and reconcile him in advance with their death because it will make a little more space available; though the narrowness of his empire is slowly driving him mad, nevertheless times enmeshes him in its nets—not the invisible, superhuman time of the cosmos and history, not the pulsating time of waking or sleeping consciousness, but the tyrannical, petty, dispersed, fraudulent time of the alarm clock, the time that lurks in wait from morning to night, that is sold for a song but dearly bought, the time that is lost no matter how hard we try to save it, the time that we cherish even when we waste it, that we can illumine or darken, sanctify or desecrate, the daily time that pants on stairways, jumps into buses, clatters away on machines and punches time cards, the time of monotonous, servile occupations that neglects friends, regulates traffic and governs our comings and goings, our meetings and separations. A man can make his peace with this everyday time, this impassive and incorruptible, sometimes merciful and even friendly authority; he can give in to its whims, bargain with it for small favors, and even— since it weighs on us all—ignore it now and then. Or else, stricken with its horror, he can die of it day after day, from morning to night.

OCCUPATION

Bandula lived here on this square.

Inside the gate I make my way under a crossfire of eyes; they peer through the side windows, through the iron gratings in the hallways, through the cracks of half-open doors, all aiming patiently at me. I pass out of their range at one turn of the stairs, but there they are again at the next; the drowned face of an old woman appears, then a sugary, forced smile; clusters of eyes flash from angles of light and curves of shadow. With a heavy tread I follow the glassy spiral of docile expectation, urgent expectation, commanding expectation. My eyes follow the banister, studying the lime and saltpeter landscapes on the wall, the movements and glances behind the windows. Someone nods to me, I return the greeting. No one asks me whom I am looking for or what I want; they already know. I am neither a relative from the country, nor a creditor, nor a peddler, nor a lover, and when I turn into the corridor leading to the Bandulas' door, secret signals pass back and forth in this theater-in-the-round; my victory is recognized, I am a soldier in an army of occupation; they accept me, someday perhaps they will testify against me, but my obstinate, unruffled progress has made it clear to them that the man who shuts the Bandulas' door behind him is the representative of authority.

As I had seen from below, the door with its ragged curtain was open. The dark vestibule and the corridor running off it at right angles are shared by all three tenants. I am engulfed by tenement smells: moth balls, kerosene, pickled onions, rancid fat, blocked-up drains, mice lying dead in a pile of musty laundry; the smells do not wholly mingle, nor can they be clearly distinguished, but seem rather to flit about in twos and threes like souls in the upper world freed of their earthly bonds. On the wall to the right, bereft of his frame, a gentleman with a Franz Josef beard meditates in grave half-profile, resting his hand with its many rings on a globe—most likely one of the Bandula forebears. An air of melancholy resignation plays about the two tufts of his beard and the lenses of his pince-nez: the world is what it is, nothing can change it, and sooner or later this gentleman will remove his hand from it, rings and all. If he were to look down, the contents of an open chest would justify his dark thoughts: in it broken dentures lie higgledy-piggledy like rocks in a steam shovel or guns thrown down at the feet of the enemy; these dusty pink palates no longer evoke the joys of mastication, but rather make one think of subsoil water and muck crawling with worms between the jaws of skeletons. This is where the elderly dental technician who informed on Bandula keeps the relics of his many years of hard work, just as—you never can tell, some day one may be asked for proof of an industrious life—another man keeps letterhead stationery, a rubber stamp, his license, a photograph of his workshop, and a copy of his tax returns in his desk drawer. I hear a sound of scratching, a shadow crosses the floor, and from the depths of the hall a tortoise comes toward me, a contemporary no doubt of the man with the Franz Josef beard. It approaches me trustingly, exposing its vulnerable parts, swaying its flat head, slow ambassador of neutral time, mute king and guardian of this dark place, leaving behind his cold feet a trail of parallel zigzags. His dignity is impaired only by one inappropriate accessory: on his back a heart transfixed by an arrow has been traced in lipstick by a playful hand, most probably the hand of Anna F——, waitress, the other co-tenant, which one can easily imagine stroking the belly of a casual customer. The far wall of the corridor is pierced by three doors, two of which are painted; on the third the paint is peeling. I press the handle and enter the defunct Bandulas' room.

2

I find the child alone. He is sitting dry-eyed in his crib, sucking his big toe and looking at a piece of bread that has fallen on the floor. He bends forward and I notice that even his shoulder is covered with white down. Startled by my arrival, he takes his toe out of his mouth, begins to shiver, scrambles to his feet, leans back against the frame of his crib, and with awkward, uncertain movements rocks to and fro, rubbing his chest against the bars, letting his long arms hang down outside, and curling up the toes of his deformed feet. A short, deep guttural sound comes out of him, then he begins to coo, in a low tone at first; gradually his voice grows shrill and he lets out a long shriek, while the tendons of his thin neck quiver under his big bony chin and he stares open-eyed. His heavy, imploring look disarms me. I tickle him under one ear and stroke his back; slowly, happiness wells up in him till it reaches his eyes and bursts from his throat; he scampers about, squealing and yapping; he nestles up against my hand, maneuvers so as to rub as much skin as possible against it, clutches my wrist, and pulls the sleeve of my coat. I rough his glossy down, bewildered by his ecstasy; he thrusts his skull into the palm of my hand, draws my hand to his face, and suddenly, at the height of his bliss, bites it. It hurts. I have to push back his forehead to free my hand from his fangs. As I draw back, his sallow body tenses; he comes alive only when touched. Behind the wooden bars of his crib his shivering body has seldom been favored with the touch of a stranger's hand.

I have brought a piece of salami; I give it to him, it makes him laugh. It gives me pleasure to watch him take a bite with an agility that exceeds his understanding. He bites again only after his tongue has swept the last vestiges of the previous mouthful from between his teeth. I expected him to swallow without chewing, and his economical method of eating shows that he is capable of a certain discipline. This leads me to believe that Bandula applied his theory too soon, that he should have tried to train the child. If the father hadn't sunk into apathy, the son might now be wearing clothes, using a chamber pot, and eating with a spoon. Thanks to these habits, he might have been accepted as a member—a somewhat underprivileged member, to be sure—of the human community. In the present case I am not inclined to overestimate this privilege; still, I myself would have shown more perseverance in trying to shape the child to the more hygienic if not innocent ways of my contemporaries. Possibly the father enjoyed asking himself the riddle: Is my son human or not? Perhaps it amused him to preserve the ambiguity, so that he contented himself with superficial and increasingly uncertain indications, and declined to look deeper.

It seems likely that Bandula overreacted to the humiliations that came his way. A novice among victims, he fell harder and the effects were more lasting than warranted by the actual force of the blow. Victims sometimes behave in an odd way: they resist as long as possible, then suddenly they submit and start lamenting to distract their tormentors. In spite of their gray hair they climb up on the table for the twentieth time and fall flat on their faces because their bruised feet are no longer able to sustain their weight; they build themselves a gallows, dig themselves a pit, take off their clothes without batting an eyelash, and covering their genitals with their hands, await the last command; five minutes before they are to die the whistle blows for them to gallop around the icy yard; and then from their enslaved bodies they migrate with astonishing haste to the terrible, inviolable freedom that at every subsequent affront has grown bigger and brighter. Was Bandula dazzled by the thought of such freedom? I tend to think so, for otherwise how could he have left his son in such an animal condition and justified his decision on grounds of inexorable necessity?

The child has finished the salami. Tired, he sinks to his knees; his tongue is hanging out and he's panting. I give him some water, he drinks half of it and pours the rest down his chest, slaps his belly, rubs his testicles, clicks his tongue several times, then leans forward till his forehead rests on the soiled nylon sheet, clasps his hands behind his neck, raises his thin, filthy buttocks, and gets ready to sleep. With his eyes already closed, he reaches out to the corner of his crib and takes possession of a black lace rag, which must once have been his mother's brassière. He starts chewing the bone stiffeners. The cord on his right ankle tightens, his feet beat rhythmically on the bed. He's been fondled, he's been fed, now he's all right, everything's all right.

Around me lies the testimony to the defunct parents' capriciousness: the fan, the stringless tennis racquet, the horoscope chart, the occultist crime novel—in fact everything that was here before. A paper bag lies on the table; I look inside and find broken eggshells stacked together, which is new—everything else I've seen before. Under the perforated cheese bell the two white mice are lying on their backs, their legs giving an occasional twitch and their bellies pulsating slightly. I push them some bread crumbs through the holes, but they are past eating crumbs and sweep them aside with their tails.

Reluctantly, I turn toward the bed. The pallet that covers the steel springs still shows the imprint of the two bodies. The ancient quilt is folded back, the stretcher bearers seem to have removed the Bandulas gently; I have a feeling that if I were to put my hand on the mattress I should still feel the warmth of their bodies. It is absurd that the child's only memento of his mother should be that black brassière. He has fallen asleep with the thing in his mouth. I cover him up, open the window, and sit down in the decrepit rocking chair at the head of the bed.

3

Monotonous afternoon sounds seep in through the window, a truck door slams, someone somewhere is closing his shutters, crates are being stacked, a garden hose hisses, a handcart creaks, further on coal is being shoveled, probably into a cellar window, the loudspeaker makes an announcement to the stall holders, buckets—probably outside the florist's clatter on the flagstones, a rattle clicks unevenly, an engine has trouble starting, a street sweeper backfires, a blind man's stick taps on the wall of a house, a locomotive whistles in the nearby station, farther away an ambulance siren howls, the doors of the movie house swing open, a tile slips down off the roof of the house next door and gets stuck in the drainpipe, someone is thrown out of the corner bar, a glass shatters on the pavement, the trumpet vendor gives a last blast on his merchandise before closing, and all is still.

My eyes follow the cracks in the ceiling. The whitewash on the iron beams is stained with smoke; where the ceiling meets the front wall it is almost black, covered with a network of fissures, lacelike designs that suggest the broken lines on an electrocardiogram, the handwriting of an old man writing a letter on his deathbed, the cranial sutures of an infant. The ceiling darkens, golden stallions pace across an arched stone bridge, on each side stand saints with bowed, hooded heads. The horses are drawing a hearse, on top of which sit five shaggy figures strumming guitars. In the middle an old man in a black raincoat, a gray-bearded barroom saint, a strolling graphologist, a toothless peddler, a forgotten musical clown, possibly a dealer in stolen goods, in any event an old man in a black raincoat, lifts high his silver saxophone, tosses back his head, and blows. Out of the instrument pour shaggy figurines in black raincoats, no doubt peddlers or strolling graphologists or possibly even forgotten musical clowns or dealers in stolen goods, lifting minute silver saxophones.

Is that a key turning in the lock? I jump up, I stagger, fatigue settles on my brain like a fur cap. I sit down again in the rocking chair and rock backward and forward. I wouldn't be surprised to find that the door was really locked. I'd settle down here and look after the child in this room that had closed around me. Never have I felt so close to his dead father as I do now. This chair was his place when the child was sleeping, he would sit rocking back and forth beside him. Sometimes he left the room—even a sentry leaves his post now and then—but wherever he went his responsibility went with him. This little body was his—it was his body. He might have chosen to cast it off, but he tied himself to it as long as he could bear it. From morning to night, from meal to bowel movement, the father revolved in a closed circle with his son, confining his effort to a few precise, simple, and useless movements. I imagine that, as he listened to the child's unvarying guttural sounds, the walls of all his tomorrows opened before him and he saw through to his death.

If I were trapped in this room, I'd potter about just as he did. I'd move my black king on the broken chessboard, knowing perfectly well that the white pawn would be queened. I'd simply carry on with the game, which would end for me exactly as it had for him. I envy Bandula: ignoring all doubt, he must have submitted to an iron discipline; in this flea circus of a room he could hardly have been tempted to look for a meaning in what he was doing. All in all, his suicide was just as foreseeable as the falling of a distended raindrop from a telephone wire.

4

The child gets going. With his right hand he shakes the crib, with the left he plucks at his genitals. For a long moment he gasps mutely for air, then lets out a moan that develops into a long, nerve-racking scream. His despair rises and falls silent with the regularity of an internal-combustion engine. He stamps on his mother's brassière, throws out his muscular little chest; a sob shakes him, and his body, like that of a patient undergoing shock treatment, freezes into a taut arc. I stroke his hair and try to relax his trembling joints by softly calling his name and brushing a sugar cube against his lips. He is insensible from top to toe, as though coated with glass. I sit down and listen, tetanized as by a dentist's drill; his tears chill me to the bone, his rigid face turns scarlet. I want to run away, or at least put my hand over his mouth, but instead I get up, go over to the window, turn my back, and wait for him to stop. He stops crying as unexpectedly as he began, crouches, and buries his face in the brassière. His upraised behind is shaken with an occasional sob as the tension ebbs away. I sigh with the same sort of relief as in the circus, when the men spinning around the wheel of death on their roaring cycles finally slow down and descend from the perilous walls, or when the trapeze artist, who had been hanging by her teeth from her partner's rope, completes her dazzling gyrations and comes to rest on her perch.

5

This obsession of mine is beginning to disgust me; I can't tear my eyes away from what I see day after day; I talk about it, I rave; this eternal recurrence is unhealthy, malignant. My defensive reflexes are slack, more and more often the blows hit me in the pit of the stomach; it's what happens to aging wrestlers who are baffled by the new techniques and keep finding themselves flat on the mat. Other people's sufferings have been affecting me this way lately; my head is full of their stories, my dreams are live with them, and though no two are the same, they are all of the same kind: I strongly suspect that those of my acquaintances who manage to live day after day with equanimity are sleight-of-hand artists. Occupational bias leads the psychiatrist to find insanity in the sane, the detective to perceive guilt in the innocent, and the gravedigger to look upon the healthiest of men as a promising prospect.

But this child, this room, and a thousand other rooms that have left me sickened with rage, exist ineffaceably. The heroes of my files solve their problems or vanish from sight, but others take their places. What can I do in the face of this frenzied squirming, which gets nowhere and regularly ends in defeat? Nothing, or next to nothing. I observe it, I draw parables from disaster, and compile records of failure. My fossilizing memory collects photographs of the protagonists; these are the people who undergo, cause, fail to understand, avenge, bewail, dread, or invite suffering. My job is to sell indifference and normalcy; I try to respect my contract, but sometimes I forget all about my employers. I am too wrapped up in the victims, and my solicitude expunges the past, expels them from the world.

I know they are not only victims, they are guilty as well. But what came first? I keep a thousand acquittals in reserve, but I am also able to refute their garrulous or mute justifications. It can't be denied that they invite suffering, aggressively at first, later through sheer force of habit. They stare at a patch of wall inside an empty picture frame; they compare their lives with what they see, and it makes them ill. They are guinea pigs whom the reward has ceased to attract, they are sick of the red light and sick of salivating. They want a day off; the printer has forgotten to mark the legal holidays on their calendar, and they dash it to the floor. They have fallen out of the present, the past is a jumble of events surrounded by a barbed-wire fence, and they look at the future as a suspect looks at the public prosecutor. They wear leather gloves to hide their wooden hands, and take them off when they want to caress someone. Parallel tunnels of love. Urgent, avid summonses, belated, circumstantial replies. Two boredoms entertain each other, two fears reassure each other, two policemen police each other. And the child—he understands nothing, even his incomprehension escapes him. He remains as he was when his mother brought him into the world, and makes no attempt to re-create himself. A thumbnail sketch of a child. Nothing exceptional about it. But his sobs . . . they were real.

WE CAN LEARN
FROM IDIOTS

The time I have frittered away here in the Bandulas' room overlooking the darkening marketplace has undoubtedly been lost time, and to prolong it would be dangerous. If there were room for him, I should call a taxi, pick him up, and take him to the home for hopelessly backward children.

I hold him in my arms; he is wrapped in a banket, a bundle of fear, his legs saw the air and his hands clutch at the air. Over my head, a tattered umbrella of shrieks. Higher still, hovering in indifferent serenity, the dusty griffin of the administration, on its wings the symbols of authority and in its beak a summons. There is no one in the corridor, but from the communal toilet to the battered swinging door by the stairwell it is raked by invisible eyes. I knock at one of the doors. Suddenly the whole maze of corridors is filled with children, cats, potato-peeling fathers, front-door-polishing mothers, and broom-brandishing grandmothers. One by one they say good-bye to Feri: some kiss him, some just take his foot in their hands, others make the sign of the cross on his forehead. I'd take the child to the home today except that they have no room for him.

The official decision is in my pocket. I signed it myself, of course, but then I put the official stamp on it. The moment the rubber hit the paper, the typewritten sheet with the official letterhead ceased to be the instrument of my will; just as a soldier obeys his superiors, so I, once an official decision has left my hands, submit to it. In recognition of my modest talents, I am usually entrusted with the execution; I myself have to direct the campaign, which occasionally involves a policeman, a welfare officer, a hospital minibus, or a spacious, black official car. I've got used to it, but it's nasty work; the fact is, I'm a professional child snatcher. Parents may beat their breasts, neighbors may gather around, the child may dive under the bed or bite my hand, sympathy may soften my companions, but I know only one thing: as long as I have no reason to modify them, the terms of my rubber-stamped document have to be carried out. I have to remove the child from a home where he is homeless to an institution where he will possibly be less so.

I would willingly hand over these duties to someone else. Last week I took four children away from a homosexual upholsterer. He had taught his children to pick pockets so he could keep two bricklayers, with faces like gorillas, who called themselves twins, though they hardly

67

resembled each other at all. In return for board and lodging, the pseudo-twins accepted the upholsterer's love; besides, they were afraid of his switchblade knife. When I was there, they pretended to be feebleminded. The upholsterer fell on his knees, tried to kiss my hand, wept, and pleaded to be taken to prison instead. He even held out his wrists to be handcuffed, but when I got sick of his play-acting and handed the children one by one to the muscular woman from the welfare office, he turned around and pulled his knife out of his boot. The young police officer who was with me threw his club from the opposite corner of the room—a direct hit. The upholsterer sat on the floor with his head in his hands, moaning that we'd tried to kill him, while the terrified gorillas sat on the bed twiddling their thumbs. The upholsterer's gypsy wife, whom her husband has beaten senseless, alternately sucked at her pipe and spat, meanwhile calling on Providence to provide a rope to hang her husband with and vultures to pluck out various parts of his anatomy. I was the last to leave the house. With the oldest child I passed through the crowd of increasingly hostile neighbors; one of them tried to hit me in the stomach. The driver sat smoking at the wheel of the official car. "What a job!" he remarked half an hour later as we came away from the children's home. "Nobody can dream up such rotten jobs as you, Comrade T——." He had gone on to tell me about much more entertaining happenings that he had sometimes witnessed in the rear-view mirror. And indeed the goings-on he described were a lot more entertaining than the endless wailing of my protégés. He also remarked that a lot of people in the office wondered why I did this filthy work. Himself, for instance —he had his car, he drove it and kept it in order, and that was that. But to decide out of all those masses of people who were the bad ones and who were the stupid bastards, to lay down the law and act as dogcatcher—what was there in it for me? "You get used to it," I said. "It looks

worse to an outsider, and at least nobody's after my job."
The driver understood my last point, yes, the security was
worth having, people were crummy, even in the cemetery
they tried to swipe each other's place. There you have it,
I said, and we drove on in silence.

My program for the day is determined by recognized
techniques for the handling of life's misfits. If the consequences prove unfortunate, I'll have time to worry about
it later on. As executor of my own legal decision, I could
perfectly well ignore all considerations that would only
impede my action, and proceed according to the law. In
this case, moreover, there is nothing to stop me: the parents are dead and buried, and for the moment I am their
child's legal guardian. I don't believe anyone would willingly dispute my miserable rights in this respect. Though
it's very late, though this seemingly endless working day
is already fading into the next, if it were only a question
of my own wishes and the rules, I would pack the child
and hand him over to the appropriate authority. Then
I'd be rid of this troublesome matter, having done all that
could be expected of me as scrupulously as when I put a
file in order before sending it on to the records department. According to the rules of my job, I am bound only
to take the unattended minor to the place specified in the
directive; no more time-consuming or sympathetic involve-
ment is required of me. I would take a taxi (chargeable
to expenses); wrapped in a gray blanket, the aforesaid evil-
smelling minor Feri Bandula, who yesterday, in the fifth
year of his life, in complete ignorance of his lot, was left
without father and mother, would sit on my lap as on the
lap of an inexperienced nanny. If they accepted him, Feri
would disappear through the trap door leading to the
repository for infantile rubbish, where with others of his
kind he would consume a certain amount of bread and
ultimately die, just as adult rubbish is consigned by the
social order to the security sections of mental hospitals

69

and prisons or to old people's homes, where, segregated from the normally functioning majority, it waits with disciplined patience for the death that will relieve society of an unwanted economic burden.

2

He would glide across the city under the dark-blue flood of evening, or tomorrow morning in the blazing sunlight; at crossings passers-by would peer into our car and turn away in dismay; up the ramp to the bridge, pitching into the wind—the wind that flakes the water, that howls around our windows and stiffens the national and foreign flags lined up on the parapet in accordance with a meticulous protocol. On the far side we would turn north along the river and follow a column of trucks out of town. Some ten miles farther on we would come to a fork, whence a paved road plowed up by tractors, tanks, and time leads between oak-covered slopes into a sinuous gorge culminating in the main street of a small village. From there we would drive up the hillside and into the woods over a dirt road, which finally ends in front of a walled castle, or rather an oversized hunting lodge, converted for the present phase of its history into a home for hopelessly retarded children.

At the start of the trip, the cab driver, knowing nothing about us but my geographical indications and the child's inarticulate babbling, would confine himself to a questioning silence, but once across the bridge he would guess the purpose of our trip. "The boy's a moron, his parents are dead, and I'm taking him to an institution to be looked after," I would tell the driver. "Nice-looking kid," he would answer, "but when they're like that, they're better off dead. That's what I say, sir, though I'm a family man myself." To that I would say: "He'll probably die soon anyway, so why shouldn't he live as long as he can? It's no worse for him than for anyone else." But as soon as I said it, I'd regret it, knowing that this was his last journey, that he was most unlikely to leave the home alive. In the swarming solitude of the hospital, he would be seized with unutterable distress, his movements would slow down, he would lose his appetite, and in the end some minor infection would finish him off. I for my part would be seeing him for the last time; how could I find time to go out and see him?

3

The gasoline fumes turn the child's stomach, and at the foot of a sheer cliff by the fork in the road we get out for air. Surveying the wall of the abandoned quarry, the eye involuntarily carves out mammoth heads, dragons' crests, the jawbones of primeval reptiles, fantastic paleolithic monsters, brutish shapes tearing each other to pieces. We stop on a stone terrace, and the child tries to break away from my grasp. I dare not let him go, because his sense of balance is uncertain and he hasn't learned to fear depth and falling. In his imbecilic foolhardiness he clambers all over the place as easily as a monkey—with no respect for the perils of the third dimension. If I let him go, he would climb up the mammoth's face or the dragon's head, and there he would be, two stories high and still wriggling his way upward, clinging to the crumbling rock and clutching at branches. Our cries would only drive him higher, toward the wind-blown oaks that peer down from the top of the cliff. Delighted with his skyward gallop, he would fraternize with the suicidal possibilities of space. Meanwhile, with our hearts in our stomachs, we would stamp around below, on the spot where we expected him to fall, waiting to see how long his hand, which clutched without testing or groping, could cling to a crag otherwise visited only by buzzards and vultures, waiting for the moment when he would throw out his arms and fall to the stone apron, possibly landing in our arms, possibly dashing himself to the ground. That is why, during this stop only eight or ten minutes from the home, I do not abandon this spoiled child of the heights to his games, but grip him tighter than ever in the strait jacket of his smelly blanket, even though he digs his fingers into my eye and kicks me in the stomach. And then, holding in my lap this brainless child, from whom nature has withheld even the knowledge of fear, I would sit down on a stone slab and light a cigarette.

4

As we sit here on the semicircular terrace looking out over the quarry, I could salute for hours the endless file of trucks that roar past on the two-lane highway, thundering heralds of purposeful speed, merciless processions of objects moving from one place to another; I could salute this hypnotically monotonous, unorganized but regular activity, this rising and falling rumble, which catches for a moment on the concave rock behind me, then flows down in waves over the pasture beside the road.

Homage to the loads carried by these clattering, lowborn, dun-colored trucks, to the mounds of gravel, sand, coke, miscellaneous debris, scrap iron, and tangled cable, to the concrete forms and iron, aluminum, and rubber pipes, to the piles of lumber and brick, to the bales of hemp and cotton, the tanks of oxygen, the sulfuric acid containers bedded in wood shavings, to the rolls of roofing paper, the barrels of asphalt, and coils of steel wire; . . .

homage to the cherry-red, egg-yellow, damson-blue, dawn-gray, trapezium-shaped, coffin-shaped, cylindrical, rectangular or streamlined, six-eight-ten-ton, four- or five-shaft ladder-or-platform-surmounted tank trucks, with their flattened, angular, or snub-nosed driver's cabs dumpily grown to the body or separated from it by a thin, articulated arm; homage to these aristocrats of the road whose sides bear in self-reliant enamel lettering the stamp of their grandiose functions: Milk! Alcohol! Wine! Syrup! Gasoline! Sulfuric Acid! Peanut Oil! Toluol! Furfuol! these last in slim, elongated tanks with the inscription framed in red steel: Inflammable! Explosive!; homage to the snow-white, refrigerated meat trucks, the cheese-bell-shaped, steel-webbed cement mixers, the tortoiselike carriers of prefabricated houses, the crane trucks advancing like enormous unicorns, the triangular dump trucks, the carriers of abstract interplanetary missiles ...

a look of reluctant admiration at the great livestock carriers with their caged cattle and horses, raising their prescient, doomed, haltered heads; at the blue-and-white police vans, in which immobile, heavy-jowled men with tommy guns sit facing each other in mouse-gray uniforms ...

and finally a moment of silence for the oil-green, windowless aluminum tombs: on a central corridor six dark cells with imposing locks, and in each one stands a man.

Holding on my lap a child reeking of urine, my head full of bedraggled images, before my eyes the kaleidoscopic view, my body paralyzed by an eternal constraint, I would sit there until the Day of Judgment, contemplating the ceaseless flow, the blind procession of goods and implements, the masks of the drivers imprisoned in their cabins, jolted to the rhythm of their frantic speed; and frozen by the deferred problems of human affection, I would wait for night, with its burden of futile communications, to engulf me in its shadows.

5

Eventually we would arrive at the blotched, peeling brick wall (the festoon of broken glass embedded in cement on top serves not so much to keep the inmates in as to pre-vent unauthorized entrance: the teen-agers from the village have broken in several times and raped the fat and totally unresisting idiot girls wandering about in the ancient park). While we wait in the softly purring car outside the barred, spiked gate, covered with sheet metal to prevent the curious from looking in, I would be taking the child's documents out of my case so as to get the formalities over with as soon as possible, though I would certainly accept if, once our official business was settled, the administrative secretary offered me a cup of coffee, called in the senior matron or the doctor on duty, and tried on more or less transparent pretexts to make me stay a little while. They don't often get a visitor from the city in that cheerless place, and they would pump me about the foibles, secret ambitions, and feuds of certain highly placed officials in our department. Then the director would seize the occasion to air his griev-ances, chiefly financial, in the hope that I, a person of in-fluence, he assumed, would pass them on to the proper authorities, adding a few words about the zeal and devotion of himself and his staff. After this brief talk I would not decline their kind invitation to look over the various rooms full of uneducable children, where every square foot of space is already utilized to the utmost, so that, pending the construction of the new wing they have petitioned for, new admissions are out of the question and it has been possible to accept my own protégé only by displacing the furniture in a manner detrimental to the other patients. Accompanied by my guide, I would then pass through a series of depress-ingly overcrowded rooms that had been partitioned and repartitioned in accordance with some incomprehensible plan. I would also look over the park, with its ornamental shrubs cut into geometrical and animal forms, the service rooms and outbuildings at the back, and, finally, separated from the rest by a hedge, a one-story lodge with the inscrip-tion Prosector. My guide informs me that, with one or two exceptions, those admitted to the home never leave by the main gate but via this little building, whence they are taken to the nearby village cemetery, but that this does not discourage the thousands of parents with equally hopeless children from harassing the local administration and the central office in town with pleas and petitions, and even trying to bribe them. Having taken note of all this interesting information, which, I suspect, has been supplied me out of an ulterior motive, I would express my appreciation of their unstinting, self-sacrificing activity, pick up my brief-case back in the admission office, and cast a last glance into the observation room, where little Bandula would be marking time on a white, starched sheet with his usual restless pitching movement, rubbing his chest up against the bars of his crib. I feel sure that my guide, so dispassionate in his remarks about the inmates, would consider an affectionate leave-taking with more surprise than approval, and besides, the observation room is extremely stuffy. Consequently I would merely wave a token farewell to the child, certain that the meaning of my gesture would not get through his vacuous gaze to his consciousness, and after shaking hands with the staff, hasten down the steps of the pillared portico to where the taxi driver, impatiently drumming his fingers on the half-open window of his car, would be waiting to take me back from this morgue, which humanitarianism had disguised as a home, to the city that tramples its misfits and castaways, the city where both of us have our jobs and families and friends capable of articulate speech, and where more or less efficient organizations segregate the untouchables, the maladjusted, the waste products of a society that maintains order by violence, from us free citizens with our inborn sense of duty: the sight of their repulsive existence must not be permitted to remind us that we and they might have anything in common.

Behind the bars: midget heads, distended bodies, misshapen heads, stunted bodies; pointed skulls, receding skulls, dropsically arched, hollow-sunken, lopsided, deeply cleft skulls; frilled harelips, lipless mouths open to the jaw, dribbling, black, drooping tongues, cleft palates; a fatty growth from the cheekbone to the forehead where the eye hollows should be, and on it a minute eyebrow, a rigid lidless eye, a blood-swollen cataract on the eye, a caved-in saddle nose, two holes in the middle of the face where the nose should be, a recurved jaw beneath fang teeth; lobeless helm ears, compact porridge ears, cartilageless dewlap ears; clayey, scabrous, snow-white, wrinkled skin, scarlatinous, festering skin, puffy, flaking skin, tensile, ashen skin that stays white when you press it; crippled limbs atrophied to the bone, fuzzy, six-fingered hands, coiled, cramped limbs with the floundering gestures of pleading, alarm, menace, masturbation; objects more loathsome than the swill waiting to be removed from the back door of a soup kitchen.

An exhibition of unserviceable, bungled movements, a radioactive *tableau vivant* gashed by light. One of them sits in the corner, takes a piece of strap in his mouth, gnaws at it in fascination, tears it from between his teeth, cries, puts it back, and gnaws at it some more. The next is more active, toddles about on splayed feet; flicking his tongue to right and left, he lets down his trousers as he moves in one direction and pulls them up again on his way back. The third goes in for gyratory motion, rushes around in circles with lolling head, meanwhile playing with his erect penis, collapses with giddiness, regains his balance, and starts all over again. Hugging his knees, the fourth squats in the corner like an embryo in the womb; every twenty seconds he bashes his felt-encased head against the wall. The fifth is lame;

he sits in the center of the room, pulling beans from his pocket, putting them in his mouth, taking aim and spitting them across the floor. Alongside him, his miter-headed friend crouches expectantly on all fours, ready for action, gurgling; on outspread knees he crawls after the bean; on the way back he clutches it to his chest, which makes him fall flat on his face every few feet. The sixth is agitated; he wrings his hands, twists his fingers, rushes to the window, looks out, shakes his fist, screams with terror, and looks for somewhere to hide. He wriggles under the bed, where a fat, blind girl is waiting for him; she draws his head into her lap, clasps him between chubby thighs, and bending forward licks the nape of his neck.

Like goose livers in a tub or pallid jellyfish in an aquarium, brains, the viscous formulas of idiocy, are floating in pickling jars filled with formaldehyde on the shelves of the morgue. The deficiencies are really very slight, my guide would say, pointing with his pencil at small, sinuous nodosities, interpenetrating strata, and inadequately striated surfaces. I don't fully understand his explanations; even on this imaginary visit his presentation is too technical. He explains that there is a fissure in the frontal lobe or a funnel-shaped cavity, an atrophied or scarred area, liquefaction, tubers, distension—oh, all very minor defects. The ganglionic cells have thickened, their apophyses are rounded, rarefied, inflated; the excitational foci are overdeveloped and the mechanisms of emotional control are off balance. Real detective work is required to discover the causes and consequences of inflammations, hematomas, harmful radiations, and so on. What a heroic task for the fertilized ovum to cling to the mother's endometrium, and that's only the beginning of its difficulties: syphilis, X rays, viruses, embryonic meningitis, forceps injury at birth, oxygen deficiency that delays or inhibits the first cries—it's a wonder, my dear sir, that we're standing here examining these exhibits, this brain matter finely striated as per production specifications for the human race, a species, as we know, endowed with free will. Quite astonishing, I would observe cautiously in the ivy-covered mortuary building, among the swimming brains and the instructive remains of one or two dissected child corpses.

We have much to learn from idiots, the blood relatives of inanimate objects. When matter accords them a moment's respite, they do not wantonly betray it. They do not abuse their meager possibilities, they remain prudently faithful to the matter they came from and to which they return. And with what simplicity they ignore words, the signs with which objects prostitute themselves. They experiment with blindness, deafness, paralysis, olfactory anesthesia, paradisiacal mental silence, and if they are nevertheless obliged to see, hear, or smell, they refrain from organizing their impressions into disciplined companies, thus from the very start avoiding the temptations of self-delusion. With what a lordly gesture they renounce memory, sweeping away their impressions like bus tickets good for only one trip, so that the freshness of individual encounter is never tainted by grotesque attempts at recognition. As far as they are concerned, shoes and chamber pots are interchangeable; the idiot is a born democrat who does not deprive objects of the freedom that must some day be restored to them willynilly. If his defects, thanks to which pain merely hurts and does not persist in the form of fear, did not protect him, if memory and imagination acquainted him with the nightmares of the future, we should have nothing to learn from the idiot. As it is, God bless this being who guzzles, pisses, and fiddles with himself, this being pampered by the blissful present, who revels in his awareness of his organs; he is the hero of the here and now, foster brother of objects, our masters.

DISINFECTION

The "master" is asleep in his ramshackle bed; I have nowhere to take him, and night has fallen. On the wall, a mulatto girl thrusts out her backside and twists her torso in such a way that her breasts jut aggressively in the light of a neon sign. Bandula liked to cut out pictures from sex magazines, but he liked the real thing even better. His co-tenant Anna F—— sometimes let him look through the keyhole when she was entertaining a customer. Now and then she would send Bandula out for beer or cigarettes, reaching into the pocket of her unbuttoned housecoat for a tip. "Don't you touch me with your dirty hands," she would say when he went for her belly. It's getting late; I could have been on my way by now if the other tenants—the old man and his wife, or the waitress—had come home. I'd have asked them to look after the child for a few weeks until I could find room for him. I'd pay them for their services, and they know me, they know I wouldn't try to saddle them with the child for good. I'm pretty sure one of them will be willing; perhaps not the old people, but Anna, I think, can be talked into it.

A hubbub rises up to me from the square; I see a crowd gather as a small man in dark glasses appears, leading a bear on a leash, probably from the nearby circus. The bear moves softly over the pavement, encouraged by short cracks of the whip. A boy rolls up to him on skates and strokes his thick fur; the others follow suit. The crowd forms a semicircle around the unusual pair, but the man in dark glasses ignores them, proceeds on his way, and soon turns the corner. For a minute or two the memory of their passage hovers over the square; those who still expect something sidle into the bar, green-faced groups gather in the entrance of the movie house, on the other side three people look on as someone disassembles a motor bike. Here and there the blue light of a television screen flickers in a window; even this square has not been bypassed by progress.

Outside the door of the bar two drunks are lying on their stomachs in protest against the bartender's refusal to serve them. Customers on their way in and out step over them with an occasional jocular remark. His thumbs tucked in his belt, the policeman on the far side of the square looks on for a while, then ambles over and asks them for their papers. When they fail to move, he touches them on the shoulder with the tip of his boot. The drunks take no notice but just lie there, cradling their heads in their hands; two sackfuls of coal would be more responsive. The bartender, the policeman's ally, leaps out of the doorway and pours a jug of cold

80

water over their heads. Amid general laughter, the drenched drunks stagger to their feet and dutifully trail after the policeman, one of them muttering.

It has upset me to see the drunks thus sprinkled into exile; their thirst catches at my throat, and I would gladly go down and get myself baptized in wine. I'd be bored without the pilgrims of the bar; I spend half my time playing cops and robbers with them. Shoulder to shoulder, we raise our glasses in the corner saloon, myself the saint, the living image of moderation, the professional spoilsport yet tolerated by all, they the acolytes of chance; will they or won't they plunge into disaster, will they or won't they throw knives tonight? First lightly, then harder and harder they strike their fists against a pane of glass; who knows what will happen if it breaks? As a matter of fact, I know. And when they report to my office in their clean white shirts, they know, too. At the moment they have forgotten ... temporarily.

Enough of this educational film about the consequences: all we have for the present is an ill-defined offense, a long-drawn-out complaint against persons and things unknown. Omitted from the official record are the following items, all irrevocably damned: the wooden outdoor privy with its urine-stained seat and smell of chlorine, the worn-down stairs lighted only by a match that burns the fingers, the dislocated safety railing on the outside gallery, where sense of balance is the only hope of safety, the greasy-haired old woman reeling off formulas of addled omniscience as she stands motionless behind her broom, the graffiti that a malignant hand has traced on the kitchen door, the demographic explosion of pillows, mattresses, threadbare trousers, and ragged stockings in the bursting room, the Saviour who for years has been exhibiting his bleeding heart on the dripping walls, the second-hand dark-blue suit in the closet for Sundays and holidays, the collection of oddly patched shirts snatched from clinical death and draped over the back of a chair, the smell of Saturday night stew and Sunday soup celebrating their silver wedding, the hair net for the wife's alas permanent waves, the douche bag, basin, elastic bandage, corn excisor, the cuckoo clock with its blind cuckoo squeaking out a time of its own, the pickled peppers shaped like old women's dugs crammed into bulging jars on top of the wardrobe bought at the junk market, the children shuttling back and forth between jam pot and chamber pot, the Te Deum of carrot-yellow spinach-green tomato-red shit after an advent of nasty grayish shit, the knot of inflamed tonsils in a contracted throat, the Jolly Rogers of scarlet fever on the children's pulsating chicken necks, the slaps administered to remove little murderers from each other's throats, the spitting mouths on either side of the keyhole, the crater of disdain in the school doorway, the brass knuckles, the false eyelashes, the cigarettes surprised in schoolboy pockets, the crude sketches of copulation in copybooks, the pitiful continuity of bad marks, the irreversible tradition of failure in every conceivable kind of competition, and then once more the abject terror of the afternoons, the inexorable cataracts when the antique toilet is flushed, the roar of the vacuum cleaners plied by industrious young couples, the clatter of bored children's heels kicking against the gallery rail, the screeching of nagging mothers, the downstairs tom yowling as a rat scuttles out of the drainpipe, the childlike scream of the rat when the cat's claws strike its eyes, the asthmatic but comforting sound of an engine that hadn't wanted to start, the newspaper with its terrifying news of a remote world where important people call on each other by plane, and of a world nearer home where someone has just got an artificial kidney, a medal, three years' hard labor, a free holiday, knife wounds, birthday telegrams, or a heart attack; the fear of aortic stenosis, duodenal ulcers, spinal sclerosis, cirrhosis of the liver, arthritis, lung cancer, or inevitable detection. There you are, vulnerable and alone, waiting; and then come callers bringing the annihilating truth, stamped official documents, knives, needles, and handcuffs; and after that nobody comes bringing anything.

This wretched litany, which, censored or emended, slowed to the tempo of conscious discourse or mutilated by a calcifying brain, might be prolonged ad infinitum, is a part of the bill of complaints. It is a painful litany because, faced with such a phalanx of decrepit objects, my client cannot approach it with drawn sword, sternly surveying tomorrow's battlefield, for instead of howitzers he sees stovepipes, and instead of armored cars taxicabs, and though he could perfectly well shatter the enemy's fortifications with his stovepipes and drive his cabs through the barbed-wire defenses of the Spanish cavalry, he prefers to quit the dubious field. And so, this evening as on other evenings, he slips a crumpled twenty-forint note into his back pocket, and pursuing a neon tankard of foaming beer on wings of fancy, sneaks down to the corner bar.

At the moment nothing much is happening in the bar. Loose-knit groups of people are standing around high tables with tubular legs, resting their frayed coat sleeves close to their beer mugs. The day's growth of beard casts a shadow over their faces; their broad fingernails are blackened with grease, iron filings, and chemicals. A few customers are slurping bean soup on the wooden counter by the wall; an old man is waiting for leftovers; secure in the authority of the no-this-no-that signs over her head, the chinless cashier is shouting abuse at someone; the zinc-plated serving counter is awash with beer foam and dishwater; the red wine smells of tannic acid, dead flies and scraps of cork are floating in the watery white wine; on a glass shelf, petrified buns, a magma of obscene pigs' ears, intricate coils of sausage emerge from the swirls of blue-gray tobacco smoke. A bearded, stooped, perpetually muttering crone passes dirty glasses to the gold-toothed bartender, who holds them under a jet of water for a second or two. By the door stand two thickset policemen with prominently displayed gun holsters and black and white truncheons. A tipsy old man goes over to them and tries to entertain them; instead of waving him away, they stare unsmiling over his head. For four or five minutes they stand there without a word, then continue their rounds.

It's a place that makes you feel good. It revives you like a hot bath. During the day you hardly existed, you were caught up in the inscrutable movements of regularly functioning objects; it was pure chance if your shoe went the same way as you. If you blinked, blew your nose, or made various other noises, it was purely incidental. Now, in this dive with its smell of slush, cigarette butts, vinegar, hobnailed boots, stew, and scrub buckets, in the raw, smokeswirling light of ticking, fly-specked neon tubes, you grow into your clothes, blow yourself up, transmit urgent little waves of fellowship to your neighbors, waddle proudly from table to table like a general handing out medals; pleased with yourself, you enrich your autobiography. Before surrendering once again, as you have done in the thousands of battles that have been your lot, you try to prove how exceptional you are. At last you are what you would like to seem—an idol, an archetype. Overflowing with friendliness, you offer your hand, seize your companion by the lapels, take offense if he won't have one for the road, thrust your face close to his, and grind your teeth. Just let anyone dare give you a dirty look. Nothing fazes you; even if they hang you for it, you'll wipe out the whole lot of them. Revelation on your tongue, death in your fist.

Then your heart is softened. Over by the window a young fellow in a red scarf is drinking brandy; you like him. You'd like to tell him you were once a champion high jumper, that you did the western roll and could hit five feet nine. The other day you played hopscotch with your daughter and in a few minutes your heart was pounding in your ears. You haven't had a decent fuck in years, your

84

belly gets in the way. As long as he believes the western roll and laughs within tactful limits at the belly, you'll be satisfied with Red Scarf. Maybe he'll tell you that his mother has cancer, and maybe you'll reciprocate with the story of your mother's death; you may even tell him that you've been dreaming about her more and more and that she spoke to you on the stairs the other day. Actually, you don't go over to Red Scarf at all; it's hard to make friends at your age. The young fellow has an agreeable profile; in all likelihood he'd just say, "Really?" and hasten to polish off his cognac. At that you would really like to wade into him and pull the ends of his red scarf until . . . until . . . in short, you don't make friends. The old black-market ragpicker makes you want to throw up anyway with that corny story he's telling two cops over there about how he won the big prize in the lottery in 1933, but a whore stole the money the same day. The young man by the window is quite right to turn away; let's keep aloof and just look on from behind our glass. It's no duller than the sight of a not-so-young woman lying on her back and lifting her buttocks as for the first time she takes off her pants for our benefit; from the ivory tower of your third drink you gaze with the superiority of an archbishop on these grimacing puppets as they clutch at empty air, push each other around, and create an uproar. What are they but tired flies on a windowpane that is losing its warmth? One by one, the gold-speckled swatter will pick them off. If only they knew what you know at this moment. But the oracle speaks only in riddles, his second message cannot be decoded; the key has been hidden, God knows why.

If instead of Bandula it was I lying among scratchy bread crumbs on that wire spring, listening as my son spat out consonants, too tired to start the day, with no other company than unwashed milk bottles, cobwebs fluttering in the draft, mice slumbering in a heap, and my tattered boots, alone with my nightmares and frustrations, I would be unable to think up anything better than this bar. With pathetic patience I would scrape together the price of a glass of wine; trembling with anticipation, I would rush to join the others in that ramshackle shelter, that cavern smelling of fish and sulfur, and celebrate my nuptials with myself.

2

In the phantasmagoric world of good and evil, licit and illicit, where every breath is regulated by red and green lights and the cult of All or Nothing reigns supreme; in that ambitious, heedless world of ideas that has no more relevance to the massive ambiguity of human affairs than an impotent old man to the backside of a whore; in that arrogant, legalistic order which over the years has crammed my mind full of painful obsessions, that order in which humanity is divided into two halves—one of which passes judgment, while the other is judged—I have stood with the judges for as long as I can remember, but, I hasten to add, far from wholeheartedly.

I am not trying to justify myself, merely stating the facts: the first role assigned to me was that of an accuser. I was not a public prosecutor for very long; I meted out only a few hundred years of imprisonment. True, that's quite a term to serve; it would need eight to ten human lives placed end to end. If I were to close the iron door on myself, the remaining years of my life would hardly make a dent in the sum of sentences I obtained. There was also a death sentence, a clear-cut case of murder in the course of burglary; but these achievements do not make my professional beginnings exactly memorable. Yet without wishing to seem squeamish, I must own that I find them hard to forget. I could not even derive much moral satisfaction from abandoning this career, for my performance compared to that of some of my classmates was pathetically piddling. Still, I was glad to give it up. My next step on the professional ladder took me from the courtroom to the prison cemetery.

Presiding over exhumations for months at a time was smelly work, but at least it was honest—the morose self-criticism of the judicial apparatus. Was there a skull fracture where the death certificate mentions only pneumonia? It was my job to carry out investigations that might throw light on the extraordinarily high death rate in the prisons. A black limousine with imposing license plates carried me from town to town, from prison to prison, where I directed silently drunken exhumation teams. Our relentless investigations brought to light—stripped of their rotting striped rags—bodies crawling with worms, pullulating symbols of perfect equality and relativity. More frequently, amid the classical smell of tranquil humus, there appeared, cleansed and washed to the bone, raising no mushroom cloud of sickly stink, the skeletons of bygone times. *Fiat justitia,* we have scraped about with our spades; *pereat mundus,* we have confuted a few death certificates. We sought out the signatories in the intention of rendering justice to the citizens who had been buried with undue haste. We rejected all complicity with the living, and the outrage suffered by our olfactory sense exempted us from compassion for the dead. An undeviating administrative objectivity presided over our excavations.

Months passed as we worked in a more and more precarious alliance with the strictly binary system of yes and no prescribed by the law. Devotees of that dubious joke known as historical perspective, we deciphered the hieroglyphics of death in test tubes, mirrors, and windshields, and were often so agitated by the indications, sometimes shattering, sometimes inoffensive, they had to offer, that the water ran out of our bowels. We were still young enough to remember the cubist architecture of the piles of corpses we had seen during the war. Every evening we threw off our hood of light and truth, the immaculate hood of the law (we were sick to death of this law, which shows its moderation by withdrawing the truncheon from the testicles it has fractured, which translates the hymn of vengeance into the language of meteorology, and time and again indulges in the dreary, millennial gag of washing its hands; we hated its hairsplitting distinctions between legality and its abuses— in fact, we hated the law itself). Then one day my staggering mind, digressing from the straight path of historical necessity, managed to take a vacation, and freed from the spurs of judgment thanks to an unexpected change of jobs, found a more grateful object for its reasoning faculties in a slaughterhouse shed, where against a white-tiled wall three rows of flayed ox heads hung on hooks. Their frozen, bare eyeballs bulged gruesomely from scarlet bundles of muscle; a halo of suffering surmounted their truncated horns; and there, in a silence humming with flies, I whiled away the time with puerile exercises in unlimited understanding.

Auschwitz, Auschwitz, whispered the crinkly-skinned Buddhist reporter, who for years had been living on a diet of apples, rice, and carrots by way of dissociating himself from a civilization that devours steaks, chops, and cutlets, rare or well done, that feeds on blood and more blood; from a world where animals are slaughtered, flayed, and butchered in accordance with norms measured in seconds. He hated this plant with its brick-walled compound, to which with the approval of the Ministry of Health livestock is delivered by the truckload and from which only their bellowing emerges in a state of nature, all the rest being transformed into combs and salami, shoe leather and chops, glue and liver sausage, which, duly packed and invoiced, are granted full legal right to pass through the gates. He hated this extermination camp with its smell of burned bristle, of smoking, pickling, and steaming. Having consulted his light meter, he approached the dripping meat from various angles, clicking his Exacta in the hope of providing a docu-

88

ment that would awaken the conscience of mankind to our relentless, feverish activity, which our employers rewarded with fifteen pounds of free meat in addition to our wages. "Our whole existence is sullied with violence," he complained. "A man who participates in such mass slaughter, made possible by modern technology, will turn against his brothers tomorrow and crush them with his machines, methodically and quickly, recognizing no other sin than waste motion," and nothing would escape from our blackened blood-caked nails but our brothers' cries of agony, and no doubt, the spirit that inhabited them.

There was truth in what he said. One blow of the cleaver on the medulla oblongata, one little knife slash on the carotids—it isn't hard to kill. Whom you may kill and whom you may not, when you may and when you must not—there is no satisfactory answer to such questions, any more than to the question of whether it is permissible to eat meat on Good Friday. Killing can be cheap, easy, and quick, or it can be expensive, complicated, and slow; the technical details are easier to understand than the legal code. Though as a trained, early-rising worker in the meat industry, with the magic fortress of the law behind my back, I could appreciate my visitor's bold conclusions, I found it hard to follow him into his weightless vegetarian morality (in a few naïve propositions he swept away the very names of existing nations, institutions, churches, and armies). If I had subscribed to his breviary of universal meekness and succeeded in forgetting what I knew of suicides, mental institutions, prisons, and other dismal facts of life, what would I have been offered in exchange? A life of grotesque, mawkish posturing, pride in my home-grown vegetables, mystical pirouettes, intellectual self-castration, a cloying satisfaction in my daily good deeds, and the clinging companionship of like-minded moralizers. Accordingly, I lost interest in the temptation of a private antitechnological, anticonformist, anticapitalist, anticommunist, antibureaucratic, and antirationalist salvation, and when at length I fled from the glassy-eyed host of flayed ox heads, I became once more what I had trained for, a representative of the public order, half jurist, half functionary. My new duties, however, were of a tutelary rather than punitive nature, and I have remained what I am, a fair-to-middling technician of the machinery for dealing with social tension, skeptical enough to try, in my moments of anxiety, to find excuses for myself, but sufficiently compliant to avoid dismissal.

For years now I have been bustling from door to door and courtroom to courtroom with a briefcase full of modest but futile petitions and of intelligent but unintelligible decisions. For almost ten years I have been watching the ashen faces of my clients grimacing in frail agitation, their mouths open with astonishment, the deranged mechanism of their smiles, and the wrinkled traces of their day-to-day good and evil. Overburdened by their frustrations, the sympathy in me has become as gritty as a handful of burning sand.

Who am I, I sometimes ask myself, that I should question them so, that they should tell me their threadbare histories? Who do they take me for that they should bring me things to repair that would have made even the Galilean craftsman raise his arms to high heaven? Where did this drab serial of misfortune begin? With the statistical accidents of their cellular systems? With the mistaken ideas that were drummed into them? At what remote phase of their past? And when I say that something is bad, compared to what is it bad? Minute air bubbles immured in limestone: such are the neglected opportunities of the free will. But even if my power of action is only one such bubble, there in that diminutive cavity I must huddle and render judgment. Don't throw the newborn baby into the garbage pail. Don't let your infant starve. If baby is ill, call a doctor. It is not advisable to tie a baby to his crib, sit him down on a hot stove, shut him up in the icebox, put his finger into an electric socket, or beat him with a trouser belt, rolling pin, chair leg, carpet beater, wooden spoon, broomstick, clothesline, or shoe heel. Refrain from raping teen-aged girls, particularly your own. While making love, do not crush your sleeping child against the wall. Don't feed him brandy, don't pawn his winter coat, don't give your girl friend his supper, don't let him be devoured by lice, don't call his mother a whore or his father a bastard, don't threaten him with your service pistol, don't send him out begging, don't train him to be a pickpocket, don't sell him to elderly queers, don't urinate in his school bag, don't leave him behind on the train, don't cheat him, don't laugh at him, don't shout him down, don't bellow at him, don't shame him; in a word, as far as possible respect the innocence of his beginnings. I browbeat, assert my authority, pass judgment.

3

The iron curtain of anonymity goes up to reveal a bus conductor holding a glass of beer. He takes off his peaked cap and shows me a plum-sized lump on his bald head. He strokes it with his fingertips and waits for me to say something. Although I know his son gave it to him, good manners require me to ask how he came by it. "He hit me with my own ticket punch. Can you imagine?" I can. I had called on the family some six months before: the conductor lay groaning on the kitchen floor; that was the first time his son hit him. The boy had tried to avert the crisis; for weeks and months he had spent the night on scaffolding, in concrete pipes, in gravel boxes by the Danube, or in railroad cars on sidings, just to avoid his father. He exercised with a rubber strap, he knew he was the stronger; when he heard his father reeling home muttering threats, he escaped through the window of the ground-floor apartment to avoid a clash. Once when a middle-aged policeman asked to see his papers, he said he would like to be arrested because he was afraid of bashing his father's head in. "All right," said the policeman. At the station house he had given him bread and meat, turned on the radio, and told him how at the same age he, too, had wanted to kill his father, but never got around to it, and that now he was supporting him. He showed the boy an arm hold and told him to use it if necessary in self-defense, but not to strike his father if he could help it. The next day the conductor was nastier than usual: he had decided to report his family on the grounds that his wife, daughter, and son made love together. Countless indications had led him to this conclusion. "The minute I go out the door, you jump into bed together." He wept to think of it, he nursed his rage. Sometimes he would snigger in his son's direction: "I'll cut it off while you're asleep." One night in his drunkenness he demanded that they do it in his presence; if they could act like pigs when he was away, why be ashamed when he was there? He tore the two women's clothes, pinched their breasts, shoved them onto the bed, and slapped them with the back of his hand, all the while watching his son out of the corner of his eye. He didn't touch him, but waited for him to interfere. The moment the boy moved, the father lashed out at him, punching him wherever he could reach him. The arm hold proved successful; the conductor bent double and sank to his knees, bellowing. The noise was unbearable; the boy gave him a chop on the back of the neck. Fifteen minutes later, when I knocked at the door, the conductor was still lying on the floor as if he had suffered a concussion.

He whimpers, buries his face in his hands, and denounces his family. Yet though the others have defeated him and trampled him for the last six months, he is determined to go on with these evening battles. It's sheer bad luck that he has always lost, and he swears he'll get the better of them yet. Threateningly, challengingly, he would hold out his face to the boy, who replied by hitting him, more and more precisely and ruthlessly. "You've been counted out," I tell him. "You'll go mad if you don't stop this nonsense." I try to make him understand that he's lost the fight and should retire from the ring with dignity. "But a father can't lose," he says tearfully, thumping his beer mug. A one-eyed giant leans over and remarks: "Even God can lose. A lightweight like you can be blown away." And he blows at him. The conductor pulls his cap over the bump on his head and trudges homeward, I suppose to get himself beaten up.

"I've been left alone with the kids," says One-Eye. His wife had gone off again with the lesbian Gypsy girl. "I'm going after her tomorrow with the dog. I'll go from village to village, from Gypsy camp to Gypsy camp. I'm going to get my wife back, and as for that damn dyke, I'll . . ." and he demonstrates how he's going to wring her neck. "Get you ten years," I say. "Worth it." "It's a long time." "Passes before you know it." He should know—he's done a five-year stretch already. In spring 1957 he had sent a crate with a policeman in it to police headquarters by truck. When unpacked, the policeman had been alive, but badly damaged. Left alone, his wife waited a year, then surrendered to the advances of her tenant, the flat-chested Gypsy girl who wore boots and went about on a motor bike. At first the Gypsy girl had got her drunk, then it ceased to be necessary. They lived in harmony, like husband and wife. They earned enough for essentials, both of them turned their minds to the children's upbringing, and every evening they cuddled up together to watch the television. The wife was plump and easygoing; the Gypsy girl was muscular, believed in the stars, and had a way of controlling the children with her eyes. Every night their mother giggled or screamed, so the children told their father after his release. Now and then the Gypsy girl would send a big, thick letter, which the wife handed her husband unopened. Without a word One-Eye would burn the stubborn missives. "If it were another man, would you strangle him?" I ask. "No. I'd muss him up a bit, just to give him a lesson, to show him what's what." He smiles, visualizing a situation he would know how to master. "Then you're only so angry with this one because she's a woman?" The blood drains out of One-Eye's huge, unshaven face. "I've never hit a woman yet, believe it or not." I believe nothing, but I nod; after all, it's perfectly possible. "But I'll choke the life out of this witch." I begin to understand, I'm afraid he's serious. "Because of the stars?" "That, too. She's driven her crazy. Nowadays my wife asks me if I can see anything at the window. What the hell does she expect me to see, we live on the third floor, except for the chimney of the house across the street? *She's* there, she wants to come in, says my wife, and goes into the kitchen to cry. I'll bring her back to the children, and after that she won't have anybody to run away to." I try to persuade him to come and see her at my office; we'll find a solution. "We'll bring her back quietly; a friend of mine's a psychiatrist, he'll cure her." "What about the dyke?" "I know a number of lesbians—I'll introduce her to one of them. Come to my office tomorrow. If you don't come and I hear that you've gone off, I'll tell the police you're planning murder." One-Eye could knock me over, but he just sits there and broods; I suppose he thinks it's easy for me to talk. Our glasses are empty, and I stand him another.

"I've got a pillowcase," says a little man at the other end of the bar. He lifts it up. He really has got a pillowcase. "A nice pillowcase," I say. "You know what you can do with it," growls One-Eye. "It's worth ten beers," says the little man. I make him a proposition. "I'll buy you a beer for friendship's sake, and you go home with your pillowcase." "Be sure you take it home," One-Eye adds severely. Neither of us sets much store by Mr. Frecska's promises. The little man strokes the pillowcase with deep feeling, as if it were the bridal veil of his dead bride. After that it will be hard for him to put it up for sale. "I don't dare take it home," he says. "I took four, and I've already sold three to pay off my debts. I paid like a lord. Here you are, Laci old man, sixty forints, just count it, when Béla Frecska says sixty, it might be more, but it certainly won't be less; when I've got your money, Laci my boy, it's as safe as in a bank, am I right, mister?" He couldn't have put it better. He lives here in the basement, under the bar. Years ago he got drunk and hasn't managed to sober up since. He sleeps on the pads they use to roll in the beer barrels; he's got all the rats tamed. In the morning the bartender gives him a free glass of brandy, another at night to keep out the cold downstairs, and nothing in between. At the moment he's in between. "He'd sell Jesus Christ," says One-Eye. "Ah, but he hasn't sold his worker's medal of merit yet," I say. One-Eye asks him: "Why haven't you sold it?" "I want something pretty for my coffin when I die." Fair enough. The day before yesterday his wife saw him in the street, took him home, cleaned him up, and gave him a bowl of bone soup. "She gave me some clean clothes, too, the ones I've got on." Let's have a look, yes, it's true . . . "A man can't look after his clothes when he's got rats and garbage all around him." "What about the four pillowcases?" I ask. "We didn't say anything about my sleeping there, but after I'd eaten I fell asleep. She didn't have the heart to wake me up, and then she went to work—she's on the night shift." "You only pretended to be asleep, you skunk," said One-Eye. "It's God's truth, I was even snoring," says Mr. Frecska dreamily. One-Eye shrugs his shoulders. "That's you in a nutshell, Bela, you're rotten, you're stupid, it makes me sick to look at you. Why do you bother to come up out of the cellar every morning, what're you good for, Béla?" "I'm not rotten, I didn't touch the wife's clothes or the kid's, only the pillowcases. I said to myself, pillowcases are a good thing and beer's a good thing, but I prefer beer. Maybe you can tell me, mister, why shouldn't I like what's good for me—would you have the heart to deprive me?" When I think of his wife, when I think that. he doesn't pay her one fillér of alimony, I certainly would deprive him. "Mr. Frecska, you'll have to take a disintoxication cure. And then go some place where you'll have to work." One-Eye doesn't care for that kind of talk; he takes the pillowcase from the little man and says he'll return it to his wife. Maybe he won't take his dog and go looking for the Gypsy girl after all. Frecska picks his nose, snivels, and sidles off, looking back at me suspiciously over a railroad worker's elbow.

Bleached, tangled, short-cut hair, protuberant brown eyes with bags under them, a large, wrinkled, banana-shaped mouth, but all the same they like her here. She thrusts her face before me as imploringly as an old peasant brandishing a wilting cabbage in the marketplace after the loudspeaker has instructed the stall holders to start packing up for the evening. "What do you think of the police?" she asks. "Nothing." "Do you like policemen?" "Do you?" I ask wearily. It takes her three matches to light her cigarette. "I've asked you that before, haven't I?" she recollects vaguely. I nod. She complains that nowadays she can't think of any more interesting questions. "That's quite an interesting question," I comfort her. "It's only that everybody here has heard it before." One-Eye agrees: "A very shrewd question, Irene. Hits the nail right on the head. It would be hard to think of a better one." "People have got used to it," she frets. She looks around and comes to the conclusion that she has already asked everybody. "In that case," I say, "drink your wine and relax." "It's a terrible responsibility," she says; it keeps her awake at night. Because even if somebody doesn't like the police, he could still love his family and do honest work for the people's democracy. People were so irritable and quick tempered nowadays; they blurt out all sorts of things that they don't really mean, you've got to remember that. "You see how hard it is to know

96

what's what?" I see. One-Eye says it's all so complicated that his head would burst if he were Irene, though of course he'd had only six years at school, while Irene was an educated woman. The educated woman downs her wine at one gulp and nods with affable self-importance. She used to work at police headquarters. She helped me with one or two cases, and I was perfectly satisfied with her. Then she took to drink. She was dismissed, but at first they paid her for her reports on what she heard in bars and cafés; they didn't drop her altogether. At present all she gets is handouts from her former colleagues; her information is no longer of any interest. But sometimes they listen to her so she won't feel utterly useless. She asks the question she asked just now, that's her little trick. Her obsession is well known, people make jokes about it and buy her a drink. "Couldn't you find me a more interesting question?" she asks me mournfully. "Do you like women?" The question appeals to her, she tries it out on me. "Very much," I reply. "Good," she sighs. "My husband loves me, too, but I've got my faults." Then she asks One-Eye if he likes women. He replies with a blush: "Not all." "Oh, but you have no right to love them all—you can never love the one you've chosen enough. You men are so superficial." She makes conversation, half closes her eyes, runs her long fingers over her dusty hair; her cracked face brightens. Worried and pale, her husband comes in; he is a plumber, he is carrying, slung over his shoulder, a white-enameled toilet tank, which serves as his tool bag. He is relieved to find his wife in good condition, takes her by the hand, and leads her outside, where her son is waiting. They link arms with her and go off to buy food for supper. One-Eye goes, too; he has to put the children to bed. He will come to my office tomorrow. He clumps through the door like a coffin filled with sand.

Holding a tray under her arm, the High Court judge's widow towers over me. Her long, fleshy nose quivers as she wishes me good evening; wearily, she puts on a smile that makes me think of an antiquated coat of arms, and clutches her scratched silver tray to her ample, sagging bosom. Her untidy, ashen bun is crowned with a white starched cap, her hand is covered with freckles, a blackened steel wire is anchored to her upper canines. She sells cookies in the market, mixing and rolling the dough at night and baking them at dawn; it's enough for her and her youngest son to live on, they need no help from the grown children. In the light of the gas lamp I see the boy sitting on the curb across the street, picking his nose and shaking his rattle. He is about fifteen, a bit more, a bit less. His chin is enormous, he curls his white tongue over it; the peak of his leather cap hangs down over his ear. A young woman approaches. He lifts up the hem of her skirt, the woman smacks him on the head with her shopping bag, a cracked grin follows her retreating legs. He is obsessed with what is under a woman's skirt. "My oldest boy's wife is unfaithful to him. I don't think he's capable of satisfying her," says the High Court judge's widow, her nose quivering with malice. The eldest son has reported his mother to me twice. "What about your second son?" I ask. "They threw him off the water-polo team because he fell in love with the goalkeeper. The other day my little niece went to see him. He'd pinned up photos of the goalkeeper all around the room, and there were lipstick marks on the chest, stomach, and thighs. Isn't that nice?" The second son has also reported her, his mother, once. "What about Gyözö?" I ask; that's the youngest son. "I've got someone to teach him drumming. His teacher says he has a feeling for rhythm and could get to be a first-class drummer. He practices on a suitcase with a wooden spoon. If he keeps it up, I'll have to get him a real drum with cymbals." He's making encouraging progress, I say with conviction. Gyözö makes me think of the parrots I've known; their owners tell me how brilliantly they talk, but I can't make head or tail of their garble. Beaming, his mother interprets for my benefit, and some of his remarks are indeed witty. First it was the neighbors who complained: he would wait in cellars for the girls to come down for wood and then jump on them. He would knock on doors, and if a woman answered, he would expose his overdeveloped penis. He has been sexually mature since he was nine. The widow pours some wine into a cut-glass decanter. "I'm expecting guests," she explains. "Is Gyözö behaving better now?" I ask. "Oh, the poor boy hasn't been bothering anyone, but sometimes the little girls tease him." I tell her that he just lifted a woman's skirt. The widow bites her lip and the steel wire gleams. "He's a playful boy," she says, looking at the floor. Then suddenly, clutching her tray to her bosom like a shield, she turns to me with the humble, terror-stricken, hungry look of a market thief who is asked for the meat he has stolen. "Has someone written in again?" she asks. Someone has, someone often does, her sons and neighbors included, so why should I deny it? "I don't want them to take Gyözö away!" Do I? So he'll carry on with the boys in an institution, if there aren't any girls? I can think of few things I should less like to drag from one place to another than Gyözö. "I ought to take him away. He's a danger to the girls." The High Court judge's widow clasps her coat over her menaced bosom. "I promise you he won't touch any girls." I'm sure she will do her best this evening. But it may not be enough. "Between then and tomorrow lunchtime he'll have time to start in again," I observe mildly. "From now on, I'll run home for a minute every morning," the widow promises with quivering nostrils. The widow smokes asthmatically, and hypnotized, looks out the window at her son, who with cap awry is playing with his rattle in the light of the gas lamp. I, too, am spellbound. "Would you be very much distressed if I took him to an institution?" I ask. "I don't know what I'd do with myself. Listen . . ." With her strong, freckled hand she presses mine. "You've got to understand. I'm old, I've lost everything, my older boys hate me and insult me, I have hardly any money, I have pains all over and I can't breathe at night, but never in all my life have I been as happy with anyone as with this half-witted son of mine every evening in the darkness of the room. Don't take him away from me, I'm not depriving anyone else, and I haven't got much longer to live." The blood rushes to her large, brown face. I turn away. "Next time I'll get Gyözö to play the drum for you." "You must, you must." She is radiant. "In the meantime I'll buy him a drum." With cymbals, no doubt, won't that be fun! Of one thing I'm sure: I have no desire to take her son away.

SLALOM

Here I crouch, a private eye in a hostile house, shut up
with a child who can't even register surprise, let alone
ask questions, in this room devastated and burned out by
the time bomb of a double death, blackened by the smoke
of memories, a room that is no more real than a house
abandoned the previous night by drunken soldiers moving
up to the front, leaving nothing behind but a muddy tailor's
dummy with its eyes shot out, a lampshade full of shit,
several torn leather armchairs, vases smelling of rum,
Grandma's wedding photograph touched up with a goatee,

a shattered mirror (propped up by two chubby, bone-white, rococo, decapitated angels), and finally, dangling from a chandelier with crystal pendants tinkling lightly in the draft, a hanged tomcat, the emaciated demon of the house . . .

it would be no more absurd on the first day of peace to fling open the windows of such a house, where soldiers had whiled away the time stuffing toothpaste in their navels, spitting the mice they had shot on the seven-branched candlestick, and tearing up the children's sheets to make bandages for their frost-bitten feet, to shovel away the rubbish and scrub the floor with soap and lye, than to do so here in this unemployed room, petrified even in its chaos, where the dubious and indefinable role of the blinded dummy and the hanged cat is assigned to the idiot Ferike, who, without a care in the world, is skating through the excrement on his torn sheet . . .

Here we are, in a room sailing without crew or captain into regions unknown; sitting in the rocking chair with my eyes closed, I cling fast to the steady rhythm of the child's breathing, unduly prolonging what was intended as an official visit. I store the divers noises of this house among my ephemeral memories; a slow-motion tape recorder operates within me in this part of town where I cannot be a private citizen, and where all my perceptions (the sound of preparations for supper, everyday conversations in the street outside, closing windows that muffle open-mouthed slumbers, the mysterious messages of the pipes in the wall, sighs that rise like balloons, the explosive, drawn-out plaints of embracing cats) are transformed sooner or later into tangible proofs, arguments for or against a decision that may never be made. Here I sit like an ally of these intimate voices, an accomplice whose testimony would inevitably be biased in their favor; here I sit, like one who has come home.

It is not duty that keeps me here. If I really wanted to I could go home this minute; by this time of day most of my colleagues are watching television. I live with my family in a pleasant part of town, in an apartment commensurate with my professional status, with neighbors of like social standing. I came here only on a visit, to familiarize myself with the environment, and no amount of cheap metaphysics, born of fatigue, will convince me of the contrary. I know all about what goes on in these apartments—things heard and seen make for a kind of bond between them and me—but it is not a bond that holds me fast. These prehistoric beds have never carried me from baroque nights to naturalistic mornings. This hedge of decrepit objects never surrounded my awakenings. Though I am well acquainted with it, neither my hair, nor my skin, nor my clothes, are impregnated with the smell of poverty, that yellow star. I participate in the squabbles of the natives as a neutral but armed observer, a soldier, as it were, of the United Nations. Very little of what I see happens to me. I have never been paralyzed, crippled, deaf-mute, or blind, mine shafts have never collapsed on top of me, I have never fallen from scaffolding, no chemicals have exploded in my hands, no press has ever crushed me, no transmission belt carried off half my arm, no streetcar wheel amputated my foot, I have never had heart trouble or suspicious symptoms calling for histological analysis, no shock electrodes have been applied to my temples, thus far no peacetime death has started out in my direction. My family life is orderly, my mother is not confined to the chronic diseases ward or my father to a padded cell, my wife is not in jail. My loved ones do not sleep with axes under their pillows, nobody pushes me from behind when I lean out the window, nobody throws knives at me or puts dynamite in my cigarette, nobody pours lye in my wine, nobody denounces me to the police, I have not been shut up in a mental hospital or been thrown out of my home; I am generally well liked. I know that most of the people in this house spend their days as peacefully as I do, though perhaps in their case the backdrop is somewhat barer. There is a minority, however, who live in a state of perpetual siege; of course they've got used to it, but they complain and I listen to them day in and day out—this minority is composed of my clients. I know it's absurd, but it is becoming more and more difficult for me to close the door of my complaint-filled filing cabinet when I leave the office for the day. Sometimes I think that spending my days amid lost causes when I myself stand to lose nothing, living amid endless debt when I myself have no creditors, allotting twenty minutes or at the most half an hour to each appointment because others are waiting, putting off complainant and complainee on formal pretexts, trusting that they will shortly exchange roles, disposing of hopeless cases with a semblance of action, making hasty decisions on the basis of unconfirmed reports and prejudiced testimony, sacrificing lesser interests to greater interests with a minimum of hesitation, using preposterous legal phraseology to drown the unique individual case in an ocean of remotely similar cases, neglecting the usual for the unusual, taking the handy legal shortcut rather than the roundabout path of sympathy and indignation, dealing superficially with thousands of clients instead of giving three or four, or even one, the attention they deserve—all this, I sometimes think, is plain fraud.

Actually, what I do amounts to nothing. I regulate the traffic of suffering, sending it this way and that, passing on the loads that pile up on me to institutions or private citizens. But for the most part I wait, and try to stop others from doing anything. The raw material I work with fools me time and again, and since time will in any case modify

104

my decisions, I try to get it to work with me. There's no hurry, no situation is irreversible, today's mortal danger will be nothing tomorrow and vice versa, today's nothing will be death. If I don't help my client, someone else will; if nobody helps him, he'll help himself; and if he can't, he will learn to bear his lot. But try as I may to encourage myself with such phrases, this child has undeniably become my lot.

3

This morning I was glued to the telephone, waiting for a line. I slammed down the receiver, dismissed my clients, told the doorman I wasn't in, pleaded, raged, shouted. My colleagues and my superiors, the other departments and the head office, would all have been glad to help me; they saw my point, they agreed with me, but unfortunately it was out of the question. Regular homes won't take him, neither would the psychiatric institute because he's unteachable; but there's no room in the mental hospital, and even if they let him share another patient's bed, he'd have to wait six weeks, because they've been quarantined for scarlet fever. The machinery has broken down, pull is ineffectual, even the back doors have closed. I hunt for relatives, acquaintances, anyone who will take him—I've got to do something quickly. I've never heard of any Bandula relatives, and they seem to have had no friends; no one could stand them. And besides, who would be crazy enough to saddle himself with Feri? So here I am, busily doing what needs to be done. I get up from the bed, sit down on the chair, pick things up and pack them away, feed the child, wipe him with a wet cloth, endeavor to comb his helmetlike tangle of hair and rake the flakes of tobacco and dried moths out of it.

I can't take him home; our two rooms are barely enough

for the four of us. There would be no one to take care of him, because my wife works and my children go to school. And besides, Feri, what with the way he stamps, bounces, snarls, and stinks, would hardly fit into my family. My wife would be sorry for him; in her spare time she would take better care of him than I could, but she wouldn't give up her job for his sake. My son and daughter wash their hands before meals without being told to; if they see a drunk in the street they turn their heads away, and when visiting Grandmother in the hospital they stand stiffly by the bed like soldiers being passed in review. They are good children, though perhaps a little too serious: they put on their school uniforms on holidays, think the history in their schoolbooks is more reliable than my stories, refuse even to look at books meant for older children, respect their teachers, disapprove of premature kissing, and take me to task, employing the stock phrases learned at the day nursery, kindergarten, and school; I don't think they would exactly welcome the idea of taking in my grimy protégé—who would be capable of biting them—for an indefinite period. If there's no other way, I'll have to take my holiday now and move in here for a few weeks. That would settle it; perhaps I'll just stay here and fall asleep on Bandula's bed.

I look at the crowd scattering over the marketplace; I implore them to help me. I feel like the aging clerk who, after smiling at his companions and greeting his superiors in the front ranks, is just about to slip away from the May Day parade, when someone thrusts a heavy banner into his hands. Now he can't leave, this cumbersome banner holds him fast; it's tiring, it's ridiculous, but he has to carry it; he can't palm it off on one of the women, or even on one of the younger men unless somebody volunteers. He looks around for someone to take it, but nobody does; and so, grimly bidding good-bye to the hoped-for day of

106

rest, he trudges onward on swollen ankles, the heroic banner waving over his thinning hair.

Banging doors. The old dental technician and his wife have arrived. Years ago they wanted to adopt a little girl, but I withheld my approval and found younger parents for her. Time has somewhat unhinged the old couple's minds; they argue constantly about who has the bigger piece of meat. The old man spends his pension on the lottery; he has worked out all sorts of ingenious combinations, but never won anything. In the evening he hides his lottery tickets, by morning he has forgotten where, and accuses his wife of stealing them. In addition he is jealous of her; if a passer-by on the square looks up in the direction of their window, he is sure the man is trying to catch his wife's eye; whereupon he tumbles downstairs, rushes after the seducer, and reviles him. He writes love letters to his wife under a fictitious name, suggesting meetings with her; on such occasions he keeps watch across the street from the suggested scene of rendezvous, and scents skulduggery if nobody shows up—the fellow must have got wind of the trap. Both of them have false teeth, and after depositing them in glasses of water for the night, they shout lisped insults at each other. An adopted child might have improved their relationship, but I must admit that this possibility did not especially move me.

My knocking on their door rather startles them; they make excuses for coming home later than usual, mentioning family commitments. I ask them if they would agree to look after Feri for the next six weeks in return for a decent sum of money. The old fellow waves the proposal aside; they're not equipped for it. He won't do me any favors anyway, because I've insulted them; if I thought they were unfit to take care of a child, I shouldn't come to them when I'm in a fix. Now he has the upper hand. He observes with a jeer that if I hadn't thrown their public-spirited complaints in the wastebasket, the child would have left the house long since, and the parents might still be alive. There's something in what he says. He sees that I'm thinking it over, and that starts him off. "That fool was always right. Once I heard you talking to him. You put up with his boasting and his insolence. I couldn't help thinking you must be old friends or that you were afraid of him." There would be no point in my explaining that I wasn't afraid of him but simply knew that he wasn't afraid of me either because he had nothing to lose, and didn't give a damn what I thought of him. "It's no use arguing about that now," I say, but he interrupts; quite the contrary, they've waited a long time for a chance to give me a piece of their minds. "You've forgotten that even an old man has his pride. You insulted us, so please apologize." Overcome with emotion, he thrusts his chin forward and begins to shout. It would never have occurred to me that I meant more to this aging couple than they mean to me—that is, little or nothing. I apologize. The old man is slightly disappointed; he'd have liked to strut a little longer.

When I repeat my request, they admit that they're afraid of the child. "He's so strange—he climbs about like a monkey." Once he had climbed out of the window, walked along the outside ledge, and come in through their window. Their hearts had nearly stopped beating. One afternoon last fall he had run out into the street stark naked. At the corner he had met his homeward-bound father; Bandula had tried to catch him, but the child had run for it. Crowds gathered at the sight of this woolly-backed child, naked in mid-October, galloping like the wind in and out of the ranks of bystanders, pursued by a breathless, red-bearded, disheveled figure in a black rain-coat and undone shoelaces. Twice the neighborhood youngsters tripped Bandula, allowing the child to build up a lead. As Feri cut blindly across the street, he narrowly escaped being hit by a bus. An elderly woman caught him by the arm and bent over him, simpering, but the child knocked off her glasses and bit her hand. Several people were holding him when his father finally came up, panting and clutching his sides. Bandula wept as he took possession of the child. At first the crowd scolded him for his carelessness, but when he enfolded the child in his coat and without a word set off for home, they were moved and stepped aside to let him pass. Bandula had told me about this incident. When they got home, he had given the child a terrible thrashing. For weeks he hadn't stirred from the room, and had whipped Feri with his belt whenever he tried to climb out of his crib. "My dear colleague, you could have me up for maltreatment," he said to me with a tentative smile, waiting perhaps for me to protest. But since I merely nodded and did not protest, no more was said of the matter. In the end, he failed in his efforts to discipline Feri, whose sinewy limbs demand exercise and who is quite incapable of resisting the temptations of space. Bandula had been obliged to attach one of his legs to the bars of his crib with a strap. "What if Feri climbs out on the roof again?" asks the retired dental technician. "What's to prevent him from breaking his neck? And if he does break his neck, who'll be responsible? You? No, of course not, we'll be responsible if we let you foist this dangerous animal on us. No, sir. You think I want to be dragged into court? I've never been mixed up with the law, and believe me, I'm not starting in now." I don't insist, for though I know they are grossly exaggerating the danger, they really are afraid. They're not my soldiers, I'm not their commanding officer, and they have a right to their fears, intensified by the phantasms of their calcifying brains. I merely announce my intention of waiting for Anna, the other co-tenant, and trying to make some sort of arrangement with her. Then I wish them good night. Frightened, they whisper and bustle about in their room. Tonight they certainly won't quarrel; they are united in their excitement, in their refusal; something has happened, they have stood up for themselves. Maybe—if they are up to eating—they will think the pieces of meat on their plates are equal in size.

5

The administration man has a long arm, but for some purposes it is ridiculously short and helpless. It can reach officials and institutions, but not always the right ones. I won't say that it's wholly disagreeable to play Providence with limited means, allocating assistance to those who need it, getting work for the jobless, new homes for those who live in cellars, alimony and husbands for abandoned wives, peace for the embroiled, parachutes for would-be suicides, and comfort for the afflicted. Seated behind my desk, I look after my departing client as benevolently as a village grocer; in my limited stock I have managed to find the article required, and I'm pleased to have succeeded in cheering him up. At such times authority and I are one; I am good because I am able to do good in the exercise of my functions, I am an angel descended from heaven to dwell among files, even though my spectacular generosity doesn't cost me a penny. But when the administration runs aground, when the rules and regulations are silent and the machinery that half an hour ago still seemed all powerful stalls like a broken-down engine, when ashen-faced people leave my office without saying good-bye and I am left rummaging mournfully in a mass of futile papers, then my exercise in mythology is ended, and what was never truly united splits apart; then I am as pathetic as the client who has just left me—and a hypocrite to boot.

Irritated by my failures, I am coming to feel closer and closer to one of my clients, a blind old man whose cerebral sclerosis had increasingly affected his sense of direction, so that even in his own home he had difficulty in finding his way. He bumped into the furniture, sometimes upsetting things, often falling and hurting himself. Once a gentle soul, he now became irritable. If he so much as grazed some object, he would begin to tremble, and when he collided with something he bellowed. He flailed about him with his white stick, and occasionally broke it. In the street he bumped into people on purpose, swearing that they hadn't got out of the way quickly enough; regularly once a week he fell on his face. If someone took him by the elbow he screeched and howled. In the end he was walking faster than people who could see, rushing along as though challenging the world, until finally he was run over by a truck.

6

Light filtering in from the street accentuates the pallor of the child's body. His eyes seem to be open; we are looking each other over. One more refusal and we shall be united. I don't put on the light. I may have been crouching here for an age, perhaps I shall hide here for years; the people I might entrust him to would gradually slip away and little by little I would vanish into the bunker of our common helplessness. My emergency exits are blocked; hemmed in, I wait like a desperate commander. His tanks have burned out, his planes have crashed, his infantry has fled, and now he is sitting by the dead telephone in his paralyzed fort; knowing there is nothing to be done, he takes his pistol from its holster, raises it to his temples, and—conscious of the absurdity of his act—pulls the trigger as the first hand grenade bursts.

It seems reasonable, even right, that it should be this child who has trapped me. An idiot I have nothing in common with, capable of being neither good nor bad, neither clever nor stupid, who with his nameless and fearless desire offers so remote a resemblance to my own children that he is no longer wholly a child, but rather a half-finished, undefinable mechanism, a ghost with flesh, devised for some purpose, though it is hard to say what. To wash this abstract object, to scrub down his cage and hand him a piece of horsemeat, to give him milk, put salve on his scabrous skin, thrust a finger into the palm of his hand, massage his swollen belly, tickle the back of his neck, push his tongue back behind his teeth, and in general reduce my life to a few basic, minimal motions; to renounce the long-term tasks affecting other people's lives, to disengage myself from complex, uncontrollable organizations, to exert no power of any kind, to leave behind me no trace bearing my name or anonymous, to abandon all attempts to rise above the modest instinct of self-preservation or the slow processes of self-sufficient matter, not to lose myself in some sort of transcendence but to withdraw from all contexts and relationships and merely to stay with this child and watch the days pass, from morning till noon, from lunch to supper, would not, I think, be a more stupid or superfluous sort of existence than the one I have behind me.

I would not go butting into strange homes with my hands in my pockets, I would not stop at a turn of the stairs, in the darkness of an entrance hall, or in the next side street to listen to some zealous informer; I would not register self-justifications so contradictory as to cancel each other out, I would not encourage them by equivocal exclamations, I would not listen to effusive protestations of good intentions, I would not exploit my scraps of information, I would not utter falsehoods as a means of eliciting the truth, I would not brandish impracticable threats, I would wipe the enigmatic expression of omniscient official superiority off my face, I would cease to record incurable woes in magic formulas devoid of meaning, I would stop reprimanding people for weaknesses that I myself share.

7

This is the moment when the parachutist plunges motionless into a space that softly recedes with the complicity of a familiar but fleeting presence. I could try on this room as I have tried on all the other places where I have briefly taken a horizontal position, where amid the hazardous furniture of provincial hotels I have listened through curtains shivering in the breeze to the steps of late passers-by and the sound of distant trains, or where, lying with an ashtray on my chest, beside an unknown but docile body, I have moved an idle, brotherly hand over cool, slumbering flesh and eyes smiling at the angels.

Like an aging gamekeeper who beats the chill trails and garnered fields of autumn, my eyes move over the surfaces of objects seen for the first time; I examine them minutely but without effort, just as I examine the advertisements in the course of long streetcar trips late at night, just as lying in my prison bunk I might decipher the names of my predecessors, carved in the rafters above me, perhaps by hands long since decayed (surrounded by blue, unshaven faces in the resurrection of dawn, my contemplation would be disturbed only by blood-stained socks hung up to dry). Yes, I could try on this room with its abandoned objects, its carnival grotesques earmarked for the trash can, with its neuter occupant who needs to be fed and bathed, with its swarm of disparate noises assailing the walls, its spectacular but easily forgotten details; I could breathe to its rhythm as though I had lived here since the day I was born; a man can sit, stand, and lie down here as well as anywhere else. My body, its needs reduced to a minimum, would get used to this place—after all, people survive in cells where there is barely enough room to stand up in or even in strait jackets—with this elastic space coiled around me I, too, would manage to survive, vegetating like a guinea pig, until my breathing stopped.

Here between these four walls I find everything needed for life; nothing superfluous remains. The nights pass on these wire springs, the days at this table, I can slide down my ski jump with increasing speed, at the end a short rise awaits me—and then with arms flung wide I fly over the wintry nothingness to the next jump. Here between these four walls complex movements fall away from me, things repulse me, and indivisible time is made manifest. Above me on the shabby ceiling the horrid mass of all my encounters goes around and around, and though I resist them, they take hold of me. I was in their possession, they will be in mine; expelled from their sculptural eternity, they will stream back into history. I dispense a gentle light in the murky cave, in the midst of which gleams the faint flame of my astonishment. Amid the dust I murmur interminable inaugural addresses and in my small, hairy companion I find an audience. His shrunken brain enfolds the infinity of the beginning of time. With his droppings underfoot, he stands in that no man's land which I, the deserter, will never reach; another being, an indefinable being, belongs to me entirely; but if I leave the room, he will forget me forever.

METAMORPHOSIS

My money is dwindling fast; I shall have to find work I can do here at home. With leisurely, precise motions I potter about the room. From a sack I dig out watch straps or garters, attach a buckle to them, and put them in another sack. There is considerable variety in the work. Two cartons are lying on my bed. One contains the parts of children's rattles; the balls and the handles are separate. I scrape the white plastic handle to smooth out the jagged edges left by the molding process, then place the light blue ball between the forked prongs. I shake it to make sure it jingles properly. This operation repeated sixty times buys me a quart of milk. The other carton conceals a host of naked monkeys. Beside the monkeys are a number of small bags, one containing their eyes, which have to be sewn on, another their little trousers, green waistcoats, and yellow caps, a third the small cymbals I have to attach to their one-fingered hands. This work is almost amusing. Still, what I like best is the press—not that this operation is more varied than the others, but after turning the crank a few hundred times I feel a pleasant soreness in my muscles. I put a thin piece of gilded tin into the socket, push down the arm that works the die, and out clatters a bottle top—stamped with factory trademark—all ready to cap a bottle of middling-quality champagne. At such times I feel almost creative.

Housework, of course, even on as modest a scale as ours, takes time. I scrape carrots, peel onions, slice a cucumber, cut a piece of bread, and serve the child on a tin plate. I like to keep the shelves in order; everything has its place— the mugs, the milk saucepan, the chipped plates, the worn-down old knives—even in the dark I'd know where to reach. I'm my own master, and there's no limit to my passion for tidiness. One of my clients went mad because his wife was absent-minded and things were always changing places in his apartment. Every evening he got out his ruler to see if the glasses were at the prescribed distance from each other and drew a chalk line around the ashtray on the table, but it was no use. Every evening he noted displacements. I can well understand his distaste for the wanderings of salt cellars, egg cups, and pepper mills, but he himself should have taken over and put things away in their proper places, at least in the kitchen.

For a while I sit by the child as he noisily chews, and put my hand on his head to feel the pulsing of his temples. Duty calls me away: I wipe the floor with a damp pair of trousers, dust what remains of the furniture with a

116

lady's nightgown, sweep the brittle-dry moth corpses off the lamp stand, sprinkle insecticide in the cracks behind the boards, straighten the piece of sausage in the mouse-trap, and chase a spider with the broom handle. The child flaps at his sides, I look at him warily and almost fall off my chair; I step down, plunge a spoon into a bowl of chopped lung, and give the child every other spoonful.

I sit at the table, write a few words in a notebook, cross out the last one, then the one before it, then all of them, and draw interlacing circles in the margin. My original idea was to jot down whatever passed through my mind, with a view to reading my notes later on. But I soon realized that I would never read my comments, and saw no grounds to amuse a man who would still be myself, yet would have survived me; let him amuse himself as best he can. And besides, why go to such lengths to sustain my shattered self-awareness? As an experiment I borrowed a tape recorder, but my tapes were soon filled; I tried erasing the less interesting parts to leave room for more pregnant mes-sages, but when I played back what was left I had to admit that what had struck me as important was important only in the conventional context of language and could be reduced to silence if I withdrew from that context. Con-sequently I talk only to the child, who watches me severely; occasionally he takes pleasure in a word, and then he sticks out his tongue and licks around his chin. Speaking in this way reassures me; nothing more is needed but a bit of sweeping—this incessant sweeping up. One day I hope to finish cleaning out my brain; then perhaps the child and I will be equals.

I turn on the radio, fiddle with the dial, get a buzzing sound, and turn it off. I lie full length on the bed, cross my left leg over my raised right knee, hold a book before my eyes, close it, and let it fall on my stomach. My head droops to the right, I fling out my arms, my knee twitches, my chin drops, a fly scurries around my open mouth, one of my eyelids opens and slowly closes again. The child has been rubbing the snot on his chest; he lets out a scream of terror, he bellows. I turn over, spit in my handkerchief, and scramble to my feet. I pull a bottle from under the bed, gulp down a few mouthfuls, recork it, hold it up to the light—only an inch or two left at the bottom. I empty the ashtray, light a cigarette, wind my watch, count the change in my pocket, talk out loud—articulately at first, then muttering—and suddenly leave off. I take a pocket chess set from the drawer, put the flat ivory pieces into the slots on the checkered field, holding black and white toward me in turn; the chess set goes back into the drawer, not a single pawn has been lost. A pigeon waddling among the crumbs scattered on the windowsill holds my attention for a while.

2

Images on images: what with the hallucinations I project on the ceiling and the passers-by framed in the rectangle of the window, I have no reason to be bored. Thousands of people pass through this square, some of them stopping for varying lengths of time. I could aim a movie camera at them and watch their progress across my field of vision for days. But even if I divided these brief sequences into smaller and smaller segments, such flashes would be no more revealing than the continuous flow of images. Consequently my attention flags; I turn away from the plethoric, never-ending film, leave the window, and let the noises in.

I listen; first lying on my belly with my head on my crooked elbow, then, to relieve the pressure on my genitals, on my side, facing a charcoal drawing of a worm-eaten but smooth, gnarled but harmonious tree trunk, I listen; scratching at the insulation of the disconnected radio wire, dismissing from my mind the image of two heavy thighs

around my neck, of two undulating sacks of flour, I listen
to the whine of saws from the cellar workshops, the clatter of doors swinging to and fro, the thud of crates full of
nuts and bolts, the interrupted screeches of twisted cock's
necks, the rumble of wine barrels being rolled over
planks, the roar of a garbage truck chewing up its meal,
the irregular paroxysms of jackhammers lacerating the
flesh of the street, and the scream of a tomato-red fire
engine; I listen to all these sounds, amplified by the
sounding board of the overheated square.

3

The door opens a crack; a roll and a pear fall on my
bed. I laugh, grab them, and eat like a prisoner of war.
A young woman slips in, turns around, and locks the door.
Standing by the child's bed, she bends forward and her
pinned-up hair falls free. The child catches hold of it,
plasters it against his mouth, nibbles at it like an animal,
burrows his face into it, and purrs. The visitor responds
with deep, throaty gurglings, interrupted at regular intervals by sharp clicking sounds. She straightens up, draws
away from the child, and raises both hands; and the hair
of her armpits gleams in the heat. Her fingers dance in
front of her nose as she tells me a story. I pull her thin
Gypsy neck toward me; her grayish brown skin is dry
and peeling slightly. She thrusts her tongue between my
teeth, straddles me, and pins me down with her thighs.
Her buttocks are resting on the palms of my hands, she is
very light, I hardly feel her weight. I breathe in her smell
in deep gulps; I don't know where she washes. She lives
in a cellar on the other side of the square and calls on me
from time to time, always bringing a present; sometimes I
give her a little money. I am beginning to learn the language of deaf-mutes, though I don't work very hard at it—

for what we have to say to each other, our enslaved fingers and those mad tyrants, the orifices of our bodies, are quite sufficient. She raises her torso, unbuttons her dress, and brushes my face with her breasts. I pin up a white sheet between the two beds; the child jumps up and down behind his bars, shows his fangs, and urinates. The girl provokes him with long growling noises, steps out of her dress, and lies down on her back. Her ankle clasps my shoulder, I am on top of her. Solemn, disciplined movements, attentive, controlled contact. At first we work furiously like baboons, then more languidly like crocodiles, amid the infiltrating melon smell, that yellow, rotting melon smell. The springs squeak with the regularity of apoplectic breathing. We fall on our sides; my left foot is on the floor, my right knee on the bed. I am her servant, she wants to feel me in the depths of her womb. She bites my wrist, I weigh down on her ribs, her thin waist tenses like a lean setter dog, her flanks harden, she whimpers into the pillow clenched between her teeth. We stiffen; two illuminated cannibals fall back on the bedraggled sheet. The child bellows, bangs his crib against the wall, throws a cabbage stump over the curtain, and chews at the remnants of the brassière. I brush the savorless sweat from our chests and hold her hand before my eyes. I could gaze for hours at her fingers with their nails like shells and their bamboolike joints, but slowly, like the mast lights of a receding sailing ship, they vanish from my darkening vision. There remain the curtain on its wire line, the bottle-top machine, the beet-red neon light on the toad mouth of the mulatto woman on the wall, the lukewarm brandy bottle in the dust under the bed. While I seem to be sleeping, my visitor washes, bracing one foot against the wall, then slowly buttons her dress over her belly. I open my eyes, pull her back beside me, reach into the drawer, and take out a few bank notes, which she drops into her bag. She plays a while with the rattles and cymbal-playing

120

monkeys, pulls aside the curtain, puts a lump of sugar into the child's mouth, gesticulates something I don't understand, and tiptoes out the door. Maybe she'll come again, I am her body; it's I tripping down the stairs on her toes deformed by ill-fitting shoes, returning perhaps to her cellar room across the square, or perhaps on her way somewhere else, it doesn't matter. It's not difficult to unite like this in every pore, between seven and eight in the morning. She slipped into the room and left it, and I am present within her. But her forehead turns green, her lissome belly bloats, her sweet flesh flakes off, and the funnel of night swallows her up.

4

I hardly stir out of this room; I am imprisoned in its stupid rectangular geometry. My body has dug itself a hollow in the bed and has nestled down among these decaying objects, made itself at home in this shambles, where it knows its way as a grizzly bear in the zoo knows its way among the concrete cliffs, or as my hand, which in caressing a familiar body invariably follows the same paths. Formerly I went from house to house like a traveling salesman, always glad to leave when my business was done. It struck me as a bad joke, a bitter ostracism, that the tenants should be doomed to stay where they were, often for years on end. Now that I am confined to one lodging and never go anywhere—to tell the truth, no one invites me—it seems perfectly natural; this is where I shall grow old. As far as I am concerned, this is the center of the city, my cardinal point; my presence elsewhere would be futile and illegitimate.

The four walls and the ceiling delimit my thoughts. Here I am sheltered: I have water and electricity; rejoicing in the thought that the rain and the cold cannot reach me, I move cautiously in my orbit, too cowardly to invite adventurous encounters; my vision is clouded; objects should mind their business and spare me unpleasant surprises.

I can't deny it, objects weigh on me. I push the bed over to the window, move the table into the middle of the room, or the cupboard from one corner to the other; it doesn't help. I could rearrange them in a thousand different ways without getting the better of them. There are too many of them, they make me look at them, they claim to be there for my comfort, but insidiously they hedge me in. What the devil do I need all these chairs, glasses, and books for? Who am I supposed to seat on them, who will I get to drink out of them or read them? Though I keep throwing things out, I still have all this litter around me, deteriorating, getting dirty, demanding my attention, forcing duties upon me, insistently reminding me that this or that has to be bought or repaired. As soon as an object crosses the threshold, it starts preparing the terrain for its fellows, for the legion of objects waiting outside. If I could only shake off the nightmare of our times, this accumulation of objects. My contemporaries spend their days trying to shatter the prison of possessions, but succeed only in rebuilding it till it becomes more complex and more indestructible than ever.

There is more of everything in my room than there should be, even of space. At first I thought it was cramped: even moving carefully, I collided with the sharp edges of the furniture; in my irritation I bruised myself on purpose. Now I have more and more space at my disposal; the room has expanded, its limits have receded. At nightfall—perhaps my eyesight is failing—I can hardly see from one corner to the other. When I stand with my back to the window, the opposite wall vanishes from sight, and it seems to me that I should have to walk a long way to reach it. This room is big enough for my lifetime. There are nooks and crannies that I will never explore, unused space—it's frightening.

5

Standing at the window, I can see the most important things that happen outside. Men leaving for work, wives shopping in the market, children coming home from school. In the movie house across the way, the newsreel expounds history; looking down, I can see the people lining up at the ticket window, or buying and throwing away newspapers; that, too, is history. Government receptions, military parades, the communications of cosmonauts doing handstands in space are less convincing evidence of the organized homogeneity of our lives than the imperturbable banality of what goes on in this square. Sirens herald the minor incidents reported in the back pages of the papers. Ambulances, hearses, fire engines, and police cars arrive by turns. Someone is carried away or arrested. Water is poured on something. Even today I don't despise such vehicles, I am glad to be here, a resolute stay-at-home, rather than a bleeding incident inside one of them. I put my head out and pull it back again, I no longer know whether it's now or later, whether this is only a stopping place or whether I have definitively broken with my active, aggressive life.

At first a number of people looked in on me, for the most part members of my family who want me to go back home. They regarded my moving here as evidence of some mental aberration. Their thoughts revolved around this misfortune, and they could talk of nothing else. Their appeals alternated between pity and resentment; they tried to move me with blandishments, familiar phrases, and intimations of complicity. Sometimes I was troubled, but usually I just stared at them without understanding; I had forgotten the signals, our little rituals had lost their meaning for me. Defeated by my indifference, they put less and less conviction into their efforts to pull me back into the world of our common memories. In the end they ran out of words. What moved me the longest was their gestures: my daughter's way of tossing back her hair, the way my son takes the bows of his glasses between his teeth or my wife persists in straightening her tired back. These are gestures that cut to the heart. But then they give way to new ones, or perhaps to old ones that I never noticed. And thinking of the past, I was bewildered: How were we able to live together, when I knew so little about them? As time goes on, our conversation becomes more and more awkward. Though I listen to everything they say and think deeply about it, they feel that I'm not interested. How can they help feeling that way when I've left them? Anything I could say would strike them as foolish and exasperating. They are sickened by the child, the poverty, and the mess; what else but madness would keep me here? They re-examine my past acts, ponder my present words, and meanwhile reorganize their life. In the end, I suspect, they will decide that all my past conduct *had* to lead me to this, though actually it led neither to this nor to anything else.

They visit me as healthy people visit patients in the hospital, as children visit their aged parents in old people's homes, as an old woman who can still get around drags herself to see her husband in a home for incurables. The invalid is engrossed by his pains, his medicines, and the trivial demands of his body; his new life and environment takes up all his thoughts. The few words exchanged are without interest, and the family is forced to recognize that after all those years together they have nothing to say to each other, that the substance of their conversations was provided by their life together, and that once that was ended, the ties between them had vanished.

In the hardening silence I watch their faces: their features still resemble mine, their skulls resemble my shaven, convict's skull; I look at their familiar, beloved faces but no longer understand their thoughts or share their ambitions. They obey laws written in a language that is alien to me. They are on the road to death—this I see more clearly than they do. When they have gone, I look out the window at them, watch their receding steps; sometimes they wave before turning into the first side street. From that point on, I imagine, they quicken their pace in order to reach the streetcar stop as soon as possible and get back into the meaningful, fixed course of their lives, in which enjoyment increases with success and prosperity. In the days that follow they think of me with a certain degree of sorrow, but half-heartedly, and probably decide that it might be better to space out our encounters. They try to reorganize our common home in every detail, and to find a new function for the goods that I have abandoned. I have been deleted from their schedules; they transfer their emotions to some worthier object and discover with relief that I can be replaced. That is as it should be—I feel the same way. If I live to old age, I shall love only the interchangeable.

6

Tender spring lettuce has come in, followed by perverse sour cherries and shortly thereafter by peaches with outer garments that only ask to be removed. Already squadrons of wasps are maneuvering over the grape crates. Full moons have passed before my window, the aggressive Ram with his lowered horns has long since fled, and in his place Aquarius sits, ready to pass judgment. I am not making much progress with the child.

I have been trying to tame his animal ways, to housebreak him and get clothes on him. Buoyed by optimism, I hold him down on the chamber pot, wait for the trickle, reward him with tasty morsels. But his feeble understanding fails to establish a connection between reward and chamber pot; he goes on soiling his bed and doesn't learn to ask. The game is punctuated by moments of exasperation, triumph, and despair; infuriated by his relapses I shake him by the shoulders—he thinks I'm pleased with him, and laughs.

I buy him colored blocks, and pile them up or lay them out in rows; maybe he'll learn to play with them. But all he does is chew them, hurl them at the wall or throw them on the floor. Picture books have brought the best result: he builds a fence with them, but the pictures bore him. As for the dolls, he beats them against the bars of his crib; only the rubber elephant is treated more affectionately— he sucks its trunk. To dress him has proved impossible: diapers drive him mad, he rips off his rubber pants, and within half an hour his underdrawers start to stink. Clothes don't even look right on him. Standing naked and hairy on his rubbish heap, he has a kind of personality. When he is dressed like other children, his deformity is more evident; one sees that his face is twisted, distorted, incomplete. Another of my ambitions is to teach him to use a spoon and fork; I put cooked dishes in front of him and press a spoon into his hand. The two of us have supper at the table, the chocolate-sprinkled rice pudding spreads out between us, flies through the air, lodges on the windowpane or the pillow, or in my hair; the sticky, dripping, brown-and-white lumps look like little piles of muddy snow and give the room a springlike atmosphere. Only one out of three spoonfuls of cooked food enters his mouth, the other two are thrown at the ceiling or on my blanket; I can only infer that he prefers his raw diet.

I don't always accept my defeats with equanimity and good humor. What can I do if he doesn't understand my words or gestures? I beat him when he wets his bed, when early in the morning he takes my shirt off the chair and rips it to shreds, or catches one of the white mice I have bought to replace the dead ones and tears it to pieces, or throws the alarm clock out the window. He doesn't understand why I am beating him; he slips from my grasp and scurries from one corner of the bed to the other. I have to tie him down. I clench my teeth and the blood rushes to my head. I am not always careful to hit him on the backside, and sometimes in my fury I keep it up till my hand is sore. These fits of violence do neither of us any good: he learns nothing and I derive no sense of relief; I am merely overcome by a sodden weariness. All in all, I am forced to conclude that there is not much difference between this kind of training and what I did before: forcing thousands of adults to do things they didn't want to. In my official capacity I made decisions in writing, now I administer beatings. In the end I resign myself to the impossibility of driving my ward into the world of obligations. He will always be a child; I have to accept him as such and let him do—almost entirely—what he likes.

At first, as an experiment, I took the strap off his ankle and let him run around the room. It seemed to me that he was entitled to as much space, relative to the size of his body, as the two red-tailed mice in their cage, and that thanks to the wire netting I had nailed over the window there would be no danger. But since he takes possession of space as easily in a vertical as in a horizontal direction, he is soon up on the chandelier, which is not fastened very firmly to the ceiling, and down they come together. Bleeding and bawling, he sits amid chunks of plaster and the wreckage of the chandelier, but already he is dreaming up a new adventure. He attacks the cupboard and the tile stove, jumps up on the window ledge, pushes the radio off; at night he jumps onto my bed or into the carton containing my bottle tops. After destroying two days' work,

127

he turns his attention to the crockery shelf and sweeps bowls, glasses, and dishes to the floor. His next stop is the coal bucket, where he lays in a supply of briquettes; his first projectile strikes the back of my neck, the second the framed photograph of his parents' wedding.

If I leave the room for a minute or two without locking the door from the outside, he slips out after me; then, if I don't catch him, he runs out though the open house door and the real pursuit begins. Neighbors make a grab for him, the janitor limps after him brandishing a carpet beater, children try to bar his way, apprentices set off after him, market vendors bawl at him, he stops dead, then dashes into the market, scampers down the cheese aisle, gallops back up the pork butchers' aisle, scoots off between legs, squats down behind wicker baskets, smashes a jar of pickles, upsets the straw-hat stall, and hides under a pile of raffia mats. Here I retrieve him (he is drenched with sweat and trembling like the sparrow that three drunken coal heavers were dragging, by a string attached to one leg, over the sizzling pavement of the bridge one Saturday afternoon in August; trembling like the mouse who jumps into a steel barrel half filled with barley, but, unable to get out after eating his fill, tries again and again to climb up the smooth metal surface, is ultimately picked up by the tail and hurled against the concrete wall, off which he bounces with a broken spine and lies quivering in the dust, until a fat misanthropic cat comes and puts its foot on him). I clasp him to me and kiss him on the forehead. Surrounded by infuriated vendors, I promise compensation for damages incurred and run home to our bunker, where I decide to resettle him in his barred crib, to which from then on he will be confined, despite his passion for heights and faraway places; I shall banish him to his bed, which he could easily get out of but won't, because I'll make him get used to it just as Bandula tried to do. I'll give him a good smack on the foot if he so much as

128

puts it through the bars. For the moment I beat him only with a wooden spoon; he bellows and bites at it, I tear it from between his teeth and whack him on the knee. This I will do for several days, every time he tries to escape, until it sinks into his beclouded brain that his urine-steeped bed is the only place on earth to which he has rights, the only place where he can do as he pleases without interference.

In the meantime our relations have become somber and complex. He has learned that my hand not only serves to give him food, to tickle his neck and massage his ribs while he lies back in ecstasy, screaming for more, but also, for unfathomable reasons, brings pain. The child is not content with being an object of my disinterested goodwill: he does not merely accept my ministrations, but demands them; every day he wants more, more than I want to give. To clean him and his bed several times a day, wrap his excrement in newspaper and take it away, mop up his urine, sweep the bits of food from his sheet, scrape his messes off the painted wall; to peel carrots, apples, and turnips and crack nuts so that he always has something to chew on; to cook meat, give him milk, live in an unbearable stench, calm his sudden rages (when he wants something different to eat, or feels a draft, or because a change in the weather has upset him, his whole body is convulsed, he grinds his teeth, beats his head against the wall, pounds the bars of his crib with his fists, spits, prances around, kicks away everything he finds on his bed), and keep a constant eye on him because fear alone prevents him from leaving his bed—sometimes this daily round of duties drives me out of my mind.

Especially on hot days. Our window faces west, and by early afternoon, when the heat settles in, our room becomes a stifling caldron. The smell of wilting cabbages, poultry droppings, and discarded fish tails seeps in from the market. The air scarcely moves, we lie naked on the hot damp beds,

129

two white sweating bodies, the one with a somewhat larger rectangle to move in than the other. When I raise my head I see him, when I shut my eyes I hear him, his shrieks wake me in the morning, his mumbling lulls me to sleep at night; when the mumbling stops and I am turned in the opposite direction, I hear the sounds of his being, the snuffling and rubbing, and even when the silence is complete, I feel his presence in every pore. His prison is the barred crib, mine is the room; I am his keeper, and by moving in here with him, I have made him mine. I am coming to understand Bandula more and more clearly, and coming to understand why no one had the right to come between him and the child.

7

On the whole I have no desire to absent myself for any length of time. I'd like to visit my family now and then, but that is next to impossible, for however indulgent they may be, both my coming and going would call for an explanation. As for my former colleagues and friends, they would be bound sooner or later to ask questions to which I have no acceptable answer, at any rate no brief one, and long-winded explanations are out of the question.

For instance, I could tell the story of a disenchanted rabbi, who, though girded with the respect of his congregation, sang more and more wretchedly before the Ark of the Covenant, who was weary of threatening sinners with the wrath of Yahweh Ineffable and of comforting the meek with his goodness. And so, deserting his synagogue, he set off on his wanderings in disguise. He came to an old woman who lay dying in her drafty hovel. "Why was I born," asked the old woman, "when as long as I can remember nothing but misfortune has been my lot?" "That you should bear it," was the disguised rabbi's reply, and it set the dying woman's mind at rest. As he drew the sheet over her face, he decided that from then on he would be mute. On the third day of his wanderings, he encountered a young beggar girl, carrying her dead child on her back. The rabbi helped to dig a grave; shrouding the diminutive corpse in linen, they laid it in the pit, covered it up, broke bread, and to the beggar girl's every word the rabbi answered with gestures. "The poor thing got nothing, neither pleasure nor pain. Do you think it was worth his being born?" At first the rabbi in disguise made no move, but when the girl insisted, he nodded. Thereupon he decided to be deaf as well as dumb. He hid away from the world in a cave. There he met no one, only a ferret. Its foot was hurt, so the rabbi bound it with herbs; whereupon the ferret brought him tasty seeds. The hermit prayed, the tiny beast wiggled its nose, and the two grew fond of one another. One afternoon a condor plummeted from a great height, and as the ferret was basking in the sun at the mouth of the cave, carried it off before the rabbi's eyes. At that, the rabbi thought to himself that it would be better if he closed his eyes, too. But since— blind, dumb, and deaf—he could do nothing but wait for death, which, he felt, it was not seemly to hasten, he girded his loins and returned to his congregation. Once again he preached to them on the subject of good and evil, according to Yahweh's law. He did what he had done before, and waxed strong in his shame.

8

If I can't go visiting, then at least I should like to leave this sleeping capsule and go down among the passers-by. I would glide among their immaterial bodies, happy to see their faces emerging from the cottony half light and vanishing into it once more as I passed. I would blush with gratitude if their distracted eyes came to rest for the merest instant on my shaven head. If we came face to face, I would step aside discreetly, bow politely, pirouette, stand up on my tiptoes, and flap my wings. I would exchange friendly but otherwise noncommittal gestures with pedestrians and motorists, graze someone on purpose for the pleasure of begging his pardon with a slight nod. I would be a free and equal participant in this dusty parade, where brother overtakes brother, or steps aside to let him pass. I would probably spend more time on the street, if I were not afraid that something my presence can avoid might happen at home. My outings have become shorter and shorter, because this anxiety is stronger than the restlessness that takes me away from the child; I go only to deliver my work and do the marketing, then I hurry home to our room, where there are no workdays or holidays, where nothing happens. Sometimes I think our life together can't go on much longer.

Actually, he's quite capable of living fifteen years or more, and no one can stop him. It's not easy to imagine our common future. I am still confining this misshapen, now adult body to an iron-barred cage. If I let him go out, he gives me a shove, throws me off balance, and having learned to manipulate the door handle lurches out into the corridor. Staggering, scything the air with his long arms, he passes by the closed doors and turns into an open kitchen. He may just stand there for a moment and then leave; but his interest may be aroused by some chunks of raw meat lying on the breadboard, or by the housewife standing numbly in a trailing housecoat. Then he begins to devour the meat, or to clutch the housewife to his shaggy belly. He wedges his overdeveloped lower jaw into the pit of her shoulder, drives his muscular thigh deeper and deeper, and just as a scream at last breaks through the woman's paralysis of fear, I arrive, strike him down from behind, and drag him back to his crib. I have no choice: if I tried to tear him away without knocking him out, he would throw me over the railing of the balcony.

Or suppose I succeed in training him a bit. He hurts no one, grins obligingly, answers to his name, wears trousers, and goes to the toilet by himself. I let him out into the corridor; he crows at the neighbors and they respond with a smile. Knitting his narrow, fleshy forehead under his long, scraggly hair, he squats cross-legged on the floor and becomes absorbed in watching the cats, the children, the pigeons strolling about on the wall. He holds his face up to the sunlight and plays with his rubber dwarf, which squeaks out of its asshole. The children jump over his feet, break him off a piece of their bread and drippings, and put scraps of food in his lap. When they get presents they show them to him, but sometimes they snatch his rubber dwarf out of his hands, watch him cry, give it back to him, and watch him kiss it; they pull his thick earlobes, knowing that he likes it, and when he starts for the stairs they haul him back by the seat of his pants and set him down in his place. They sit down beside him and read their lessons to him, knowing that he has a passion for articulated speech; sometimes they tell him their troubles and he wails as though he understood. Occasionally I look out at him and nod approvingly or call him in; obediently he trudges after me, gobbles up a bowl of gruel, wipes the bowl clean with his fingers, and retiring to his den falls asleep.

Whether it will be this way or that way I don't know; I don't give the matter much thought, because it seems unlikely that he will become either the terror or the pet of the house; no doubt some infectious disease will carry him away, probably with inexplicable speed. Two or three hours after his death, I shall lock the room, hand the key to the janitor, take what is left of my money, buy some new clothes, go to the baths, and thus renewed, return to my family. If they accept me I'll stay with them, and carry on where I left off.

9

The child is alive, he is five, and I am here beside him. He's crying again, shaken by long-drawn-out sobs. Sitting in one corner of his bed, he holds up his face and closes his eyes; the blood rushes to his head, his jaw falls slack, and he bellows with terrifying composure. He builds himself a castle with his tears, and settles down in the middle of it. This is his masterpiece; he couldn't do better if you scraped his testicles with a knife. His tears chill me to the bone, he is the high priest of lamentation, I can't even feel sorry for him any more; if he goes on much longer he will convert me to his religion. For fear that I myself will start bawling, I stuff my ears with candle wax, but that hardly takes the edge off the clamor. I can neither work nor sleep, my hands and feet are drenched sponges, and there is no escape for me. If I leave the building and go out on the sidewalk, I still hear him crying. I can't stay long, and when I come home I find him as I left him, though perhaps he has slept a little in between to replenish his strength. I try everything, I put food in front of him, but he doesn't even notice it; I offer him something to drink, but he knocks away the glass; I clown and make faces, but he doesn't even look at me. I tie a scarf around his neck and he tears it off. I twist a towel around his head; the veins on his neck darken, but he goes on bellowing. Even if I buried him in the ground it wouldn't stop him. My brain is in a whirl, I clap my hand over his mouth and gasp out oaths, I hit him so hard the neighbors must surely hear. Terrified, he looks at me, quietly gagging with astonishment, then presses his face against the sheet and starts in again with incredible inten-sity. In alarm, I surrender and sit down beside him. He screams like a jet engine before takeoff, when the plane stops on the runway, works itself up to a higher and higher pitch, then once in the air settles down to a steady, even droning; but the child uses this plateau only to gather strength—from there his cries bound into ever higher regions. Then suddenly he stops, falls asleep for a while, then sits up and smiles. I take him in my arms, he nestles against me; if I didn't hold his head it would slump forward. We look out the window, I tickle the soles of his feet, and with the meekness of a dog returned home after long wanderings he blinks at me. He's had his revenge, it's all over, everything's all right.

10

A curt rap on the door, and my successor and former assistant walks in without waiting for my reply. "Mr.——?" he inquires, and scrutinizes my face, painstakingly comparing my features with his recollections. Once satisfied that I am indeed myself, he shakes my hand with the exaggerated affability that a man who has been quietly going about his daily affairs shows an old friend who has been released under an amnesty: how splendid that they've let him out, but how seedy he looks; maybe he had a bath before leaving the prison, but it wouldn't hurt him to take another, and really, someone ought to lend him a shirt. Giving the child no more than a quick sidelong glance, he turns his back on him, sits down, casts a tactfully superficial glance at the curiosities that people the room, and without giving me time to open my mouth, starts talking about the office I have left behind. I don't mind listening to him. His little stories seem rather unreal; for me the movements of the five-story building had ceased. Cataleptic officials are sitting there with dead telephone receivers, on the desks before them lie ballpoint pens and buttered rolls; the fixity of the image lends mysterious meaning to their congealed activity. The visitor's words set the film in motion: this one has been given a bonus, that one has got divorced, so-and-so has received a written warning about lateness, X is waiting for a histological report, Y has been made chief clerk, Z has been seen in a dark street arm in arm with his secretary. Smells come to life, cologne, tobacco smoke, garlic sausage sandwiches for the morning snack; already I am on the long circular corridor, passing the windows of other departments, plucking half sentences from telephone conversations, witty greetings, fragments of gossip, asthmatic puffings, "My stockings got caught on that beastly nail again," "Come on, have one of mine," "Is the clock slow or is it only quarter past three on your watch, too?"

"Why have you come?"

"To see how you are getting on with the child."

"With the child?"

"Yes, how are you coming with him?"

"What is it to you?"

"I've temporarily taken over your work."

"You've come to check up on me?"

"I wouldn't say that, just to have a look around and have a little talk. We miss you in the office."

"As you can see, I'm living with the child the same as his father did. I keep him going, the days go by."

"Is that his bed?"

"Yes, it's dirty—I can't be cleaning it up every minute."

"The days are getting cooler."

"I can't dress him, it's impossible."

I explain why. He listens, at a loss for what to say, as I used to listen to my clients when they were trying to explain why their sheets were coated with grease, or why they hid in trash cans to eavesdrop, or why they tattooed obscene pictures on their children's backs. I pour out meaningless details, talk louder than usual, throw a burning match into a celluloid box.

"You seem rather nervous."

"Why should I be nervous?"

"Well, it must be hard getting used to such conditions."

"I am used to them; don't worry, we're all right."

"Does the child give you much trouble?"

"No, he can be very lovable."

"I see, but you're bound to lose patience with him sometimes. He doesn't understand what you say."

A skillful ruse—he expects me to unburden myself, to describe the child as a little monster, an intractable animal that can be dealt with in only one way. He would nod sagely, express his agreement, then say casually, "So you find that you have to beat him?" With my stupider clients I myself have drawn admissions in the same way.

"Has somebody reported me? To you?"

"Not to me, but to the complaints office. They sent the letter on to the director with a nastily worded note. It's in the chief's drawer now."

"Was it written by the old couple in the next room?"

"I don't know who wrote it, but several people in the house signed it."

"What do they say?"

"That you, who are supposed to be protecting the child, are treating him just as Bandula did, as if it weren't human. That you keep it in a cage and beat it and let it cry for hours on end, that you don't speak to anyone, that you've let yourself go, that a deaf-mute Gypsy girl comes to see you, and that you have sexual relations in front of the child. I'm only telling you what was in the letter. It was unpleasant. Our people don't want you to stay here. They don't understand. Neither does the ministry. They demand an explanation."

"Do you understand?"

"No, I don't."

"You'd do the same thing in my place."

"Maybe, but I wouldn't have come to live here."

"The way things turned out, I couldn't help myself."

"No one asked you to."

"I suppose you think I'm mad."

"In this profession, as you yourself once said, a man soon stops being surprised at anything."

"Now that you've got my job, can't you understand why I came here?"

"I can imagine why. But that's all. You can't make yourself responsible for everyone who needs help. If you give one person everything, you'll have nothing left for the rest."

"That's my affair. I've done my best."

"And you think it's good enough."

"Enough for me. I can't do more. Some things just can't be distributed. Even a whore takes a vacation now and then."

"Sheer weakness. If she's a whore, it's because she's agreed to distribute herself."

"If you understand that, it's dishonest of you not to draw the logical conclusion."

"Who's going to pass judgment on me if I don't? I'm just a middle-rank official. The windbags who make twice as much with a quarter as much work? Or you, who've made yourself ridiculous, walked out on your family, walked out on us, and in the end accomplished nothing with the child? Just tell me this, who has the slightest right to reproach me? When the old man asked me why you did this, I said you had lost your mind but that you'd soon recover and get back to your job."

"I'm staying right here."

"Maybe so. The child certainly isn't. We've found him a place at the home, and you're to take him there tomorrow."

"You know perfectly well that I won't."

"Then I'll take him myself."

"I won't let him go."

"Don't be a fool—do you want me to come with a cop?"

He gets up, walks around the room, eyes the child, the sheeting hanging from the wire, the crockery on the shelf, my shirt on the hook, the food in the pot. He pats the child on the head and plays with him. He's relieved. He's got the

hard part over with, now he feels at home. I'm only a visitor;
if I were standing, he'd probably offer me a chair. He picks
up a buckle and a monkey, and drops them back into the
sack.

"Did they pay you for these?"

"Not much. Enough to get along on."

"It was the old man who arranged for them to give you
work. If he hadn't put in a word, they wouldn't have paid
you half as much."

"Nice of him."

"He only wanted to give you time."

"Time for what?"

"To stop all this nonsense on your own accord. It annoys
him to see a good worker like you wasting months of his
time on a sanctimonious obsession. Sometimes he flies into
a rage. 'We appreciate his work, we like him, we give him
an apartment, and then what does he do? He moves into a
pigsty to wipe an idiot kid's behind.' Sometimes he won't
even let anyone mention your name, but then he starts in
all over again. A few days ago he made a decision in your
case."

I retreat into the corner.

"Your boss has no call to make decisions in my case."

"Take it easy. He's your boss, too. He's kept your job
for you. You're on unpaid leave. The old man may not be
very bright, but he's done your thinking for you lately."

"I'm not going back."

"Where will you go?"

"I'm staying here."

"You can't. Tomorrow we're taking the child away, and
you'll have to move. You won't have any more monkeys and
cymbals, they're needed for the disabled. All this nonsense
is finished; it would be absurd to go on with it."

"Your boss has it all worked out."

"Exactly. They're all waiting for you, your room, your

desk, your clients. Your family's waiting for you, too. The old man has had a talk with your wife."

"What would happen if I refused?"

"Listen to me. You know the old man. It would really look weird. Everyone would think so. The chief medical officer thinks you need a thorough examination. In the mental hospital."

"How long would that take?"

"It all depends. A few weeks—with treatment it might be longer."

"In what department?"

"In your case, I think it would have to be the confined section."

"So that if I refuse to go back to the office, it means I'm insane?"

"You yourself know that in mental disturbances it's hard to draw the line between the normal and the pathological."

"So what do you advise?"

"As your colleague and friend, I respectfully suggest that you deliver the child tomorrow and go home to your family. In a few days, when you've had a good rest, report to the old man. We've even kept your nameplate. By the time you get there, it'll be back on the door."

Hat in hand and dragging his rheumatic leg, my visitor slips out of the room, as though leaving the bedside of a sick friend who had fallen asleep after a long talk. Suddenly he turns, as though fearing a stab in the back, and thrusting his left hand into his pocket, casts a slantwise look at the child, the cartons, and me. He smiles apologetically, blows a little cloud of sparks from the pipe in his palm, and stands a while with his hand on the door handle as if he were going to say something. I make a gesture, signifying: never mind, we all have our own ideas, it's all a lot of nonsense, nothing lasts forever. The elongated face between two showers of sparks, the rabbit-skin hat reaching down to the bridge of the nose, are gone; nothing remains but the door, the clutter, the child, and myself, and even that only until tomorrow morning.

11

Within the massive-walled building with its block-sized hexagonal yard, in this converted barracks girt with its patched-up cornices, on the ground floor of the left wing of the hospital, gray from the start but now soot-blackened and sprinkled with white pockmarks where bullet holes have been plastered over, some eight paces from one corner of the yard, behind the crenellated brick walls of the exercise yard, there are two adjoining rooms and a lateral corridor

reserved for male mental cases

of this security ward

whose windows facing the street

are covered by a dusty, densely woven netting of steel wire, while from the corridor windows, which had to be reduced in height when the piles on which the building rests sank in the unstable terrain, nothing can be seen but a small patch of the exercise yard wall and the crowns of the plane trees growing in it . . .

of this security ward

which harbors thirty patients to a room (some have been here for three weeks, others for twenty years) in tattered, buttonless, flapping pajamas, clutching at their trousers to keep them up and occasionally letting them fall down, where huddling side by side on long, low benches they munch bread, where they mark time behind the handleless door at the end of the corridor or stare at the tops of the plane trees through the greasy nose and forehead marks on the windowpane, where they bounce their heads rhythmically against the mattresses of the short-legged iron beds, where they loop around and around as they take their ritual walk in the free area behind the door ...

of this security ward

where the passage of time can be hastened by card games when the nurses let the more lucid patients join in, or by cigarettes, when an occasional relative supplies a pack or two or a well-favored comrade hands over a burning butt, by washing the chronic diarrhea cases, by picking at long toenails, by cadging and hoarding bread crumbs, by masturbating individually, in pairs, or in groups, by chewing slippers, by smiling beatifically for hours on end, by urinating every half hour, by pillow fighting, by drawing pictures of centipedes, by hiding saliva-coated photographs, by deciphering harrowing messages, by composing speeches for the doctor that in the end are always swallowed down, by fanatically counting the toots of the auto horns outside, by cowering against the wall in unbroken silence, by humming old tunes hour after hour, by projecting oneself into a realm beyond the self-annihilation of the dictionary, a realm where the continuous movie never stops and the ghostly movements of one's fellow inmates vanish from sight; all this in a darkened room lighted only by blackout bulbs, while the doctors make their rounds, while the dead are carried away, under the water faucet and even under the blanket they gag you with, until the moment when ten thousand volts from the electrostimulator explode like lightning in your brain ...

of this security ward,

where I may end up—I am mortally afraid.

IT'S ALL
SO SIMPLE

A long day full of temptation; it might have been better
to take full advantage of my opportunities. Wandering in
the maze of the future conditional with its mutually contradictory arrows, I encounter—apart from such unattrac-
tive possibilities as hastening my death and shutting out
consciousness—only what I am now, to wit, an overworked,
indifferently paid civil servant, neither old nor young,
ranking somewhere in the middle of the established order
of power and prestige, a law-abiding family man with his
fantasies; a man whose job it is to concern himself with

people and consequently to weigh conventions against reality, legal principles against society, expectations against human limitations; a man who would like to forget both those he supervises and those who supervise him.

Tormented by my limited prognostications, by the long series of images resulting from my exercises in probability and by my extraordinary adventure, stretched out on this bed still moist with the sweat of a couple buried at public expense, watching over the slumbers of a little idiot boy, I see my limitations more clearly. I shall have to go on quietly with my role compounded of fear and a degree of authority, signing in every morning a few minutes before the bell, processing the pile of documents on my desk in accordance with the prevailing rules and regulations, dragging struggling runaway boys to the official car, hauling disheveled mothers out of bars where they have been trying their hand at whoring, shouting at inveterate rowdies who when seated at my desk bare their tattooed chests and snarl through the gaps in their teeth, irritably drawing my curtain to shut out the curious glances of endlessly waiting clients, dispatching files by absurdly roundabout routes to reduce my backlog of work, rejecting just but impossible requests on devious grounds, driving away helpless old-age pensioners whose problems lie outside my jurisdiction, forwarding instructions and memoranda through strictly official channels, banishing all private concerns from my voluntarily prolonged working day, holding my temper in check, shaving and putting on a clean shirt every morning, attending my colleagues' birthday celebrations, intentionally mixing information and concealment in written reports to my superiors, muttering an occasional "yes" in response to the floods of words that pour over me, dozing at conferences only if I have managed to seat myself in some obscure corner, applauding with the rest when the sweating speaker sits down, striding up to the platform with a smile to collect a handshake, a certificate of commendation, and the bonus that will at last buy my eldest son a new coat, remembering during telephone calls that the blind old switchboard operator is likely to switch on his tape recorder, noting who has got a raise, whom my superiors avoid saying good morning to, who has volunteered for civil defense work, who is looking after the building on public holidays, whom the chairman has invited on a shooting party and to whom he entrusts confidential files. I shall also have to take some account of the usual jealousies and resentments, secrets and denunciations, alliances and betrayals, seductions and desertions. In short, I shall have to dig in behind my desk.

I observe this estimable civil servant, who is trying to get ahead. I really ought to tell him to leave well enough alone, that he will never be a saint or even a first-rate clown, that the best he can do is settle down quietly in some hole until someone pulls him out of it. If he can't keep quiet, he should just speak up for his clients: in rooms where many people are bored together, he might from time to time capture their attention for as much as ten or fifteen minutes. Of course it would be in better taste not to try. I ought to explain to him that after ten years he would do better to go through the routine motions and put up with the routine humiliations in silence, to make his pleasant or unpleasant decisions with a minimum of fuss, to think twice before sacrificing one of two conflicting interests, to provoke an occasional bottleneck in the usual traffic of false excuses. If thus, wary and alert, he can curb his sense of power, I ought to tell him, he should be able to worry through until his superiors retire him on grounds of premature mental decline, mitigating his loss with a modest pension.

2

Accompanied by a customer, Anna F——, waitress and occupant of the third room, turns and enters the square.

She, I've decided, will look after the child for six weeks. She approaches unsuspectingly; how can she know that I am going to change her life because I can't change my own? For ten years she has been a client of mine—that must add up to a month of my life—now she can pay me back. Gratitude alone would not induce her to look after the child for six weeks, even if I make up for her loss of income out of public funds; but maybe we could make a deal: in return for her services I could have the room vacated by the Bandulas assigned to her. That in turn would involve retrieving her own child for her, but I'd be only too glad to do so; she can bring it up more cheaply than the state. On the other hand, the child ought to have a father; fine, once she has an apartment, I'll marry her off to some deserving widower. Then again, a married woman with a child oughtn't to whore on the side. Ergo, Anna F—— will become a model house-wife, though at the moment I don't think she's much inclined in that direction. And if the business angle doesn't convince her, fear should help. Anna F—— owes the state a lot of money for the child; I could have her wages attached, or call her morals to the attention of the authorities. I feel sure that she'll accept my attractive and high-minded offer. Now she's standing in the doorway with her customer, still carefree and giggling. She does this kind of thing remarkably well, but, with some regret I admit, I'll make her give it up. It's all so simple when you stop to think of it.

I think of you often, Anna; after all, you're one of my oldest clients. After ten years of mutual irritation, we have certain things in common. We have entered into so many alien lives, you to be sure rather more submissively than necessary, I rather more domineeringly. Sitting on the other side of my desk, you traced figures of eight around your childlike breasts while your aunt was telling me how you became an orphan. At the point where your father in his jealousy beat your mother to death with a fence post in your house outside the village, you spoke up: "Mother was very pretty," you said. "She was pleased that the teacher had taken such a liking to her. But you see, sir, Father had an ugly temper, and drank a good deal, like all miners. Down in the mine shaft he got the idea that Mother didn't want him any more because his nails were black and his eyes all yellow with the coal dust." At that moment, I noticed your slanting eyes, your kidney-shaped mouth, and pointed ears. Though I entrusted you to the care of your aunt, I had a feeling that I hadn't seen the last of you.

Two years later you were sitting there again, inspecting your smooth knees as your aunt listed your sins, how you wandered about every evening, wagging your bottom and smiling at men in the streets, and how a stranger had once given you a bracelet. "It's my no-good sister's blood in her," was her closing summary. You had been odd from the first, grinding your teeth and screaming in your sleep, and in a fit of rage you'd hit your uncle on the head with a ruler.

The next day I took you to a psychiatrist; I had no precise idea, only a vague hunch. Drugged with Evipal, you denounced your uncle. "Little wildcat," he had called you when you were alone together. He pulled you down on his lap, slipped his hands between your thighs, fingered about till you broke out in gooseflesh, breathed down your neck, and said: "I'll take you to Luna Park and let you ride on the roller coaster all afternoon if you let me bite your bottom." Lying on your stomach, you let him; all the while you watched in the mirror and saw how his nostrils dilated and his upper lip curled back over his gums. Then it came to you that you'd gone beyond the roller-coaster stage. "Give me forty forints and you can bite me all over. If you don't, I'll tell Aunt," you said. Your uncle paid up, bit you all over, and you bought a bead necklace. "Pretty little slut," said the psychiatrist before you woke up, "she's worth more than fifty forints; she'll be a first-class whore, a luxury article." "Are you sure?" I asked. "If she doesn't lose her looks. Then she'll be only second or third class, and they'll pick her up if she doesn't watch out." I hoped he was wrong, but he wasn't, though your looks did fall off a bit. Her parents' death, I said in your defense, must have been a great shock to her. Whereupon the old man got you to tell us about your father's death.

You told the story calmly, in great detail, as if you were still talking about your uncle. After your father had killed your mother and the scream brought you in from the garden, when you saw your mother lying on the floor with two thin trickles of blood on her shattered temples, you ran after your father—you knew there was nothing more to be done for her. He was hurrying down the deserted highway; he tried to chase you away when he saw you, but you kept after him. He turned off the road, threw mud at you, and made for the pond. He didn't stop at the bank, but waded right in. It had been a dry summer, the water was low and only reached to your father's armpits. There he stood in the still water, shaking his head. Then he saw you, and turned back. When he came out, his body was covered with water weeds and his legs plastered with muck. On the bank he threw you a roll of wet hundred-forint notes. You picked them up and ran after him. He was running across the cow pasture toward the railroad tracks; a freight train was approaching. He got there a few seconds before the engine. Leaping as though trying to turn a somersault, he dove under the wheels. Headless, his body toppled down off the embankment. You touched him, but quickly let go as he kicked out. "Everything was all right, and then suddenly one afternoon this happened. Stupid, isn't it? One day my husband will kill me, too; men will always go for me."

Your uncle was arrested, and you were sent first to an orphanage, then—because you wet your bed every night—to a home for handicapped children. One afternoon I visited you there, in what had formerly been a poorhouse. You sat before me in a dark-blue smock buttoned up to the neck. In the teacher's presence you kept saying you were all right.

When I took you out to the café, you told me how twice every
night you and your twenty-eight sleep-drugged companions
were wakened by bells; then you had to go over to the buckets that were lined up on the stone floor in the middle of the
badly heated dormitory; and even so your bed was sopping
wet when you woke up in the morning. The little ones were
fond of you, you taught them to read and write and they
kissed you on the arms, but the other day one of them had
stuck her pen in your backside. You can still see the mark,
you said. "I'm sick of bedwetting and slaps and fighting
with the boys when they try to corner us in the attic. I hate
fools. One time two girls escaped through the skylight with
nothing on but a blanket. They were brought back that same
night. If I got away, they wouldn't catch me." You asked
if I had a wife, because you wanted to move in with me;
then you'd stop wetting your bed. My son had just been born
at the time. "Too bad you're married," you said, and asked
for a picture of my wife, which you looked at with approval
and gave back without a word. "Now catch me if you can,"
you said, and shot off down a side street. I waited for you to
come back, but you ran straight on. I hardly know which of
us was the more exhausted by the time I caught up with you.
An old woman urged me to slap you; a child shouldn't make
a fool of its father. "It's me that's expecting his child," you
retorted, and gave me your arm. On the way back you
asked: "If I run away, will you look for me?" "Either I or
someone else—in any case we'll look for you," I said.

You were fifteen when I had to get you out of a Gypsy
camp in the country. My husband, you said, pointing at a
half-grown boy. The husband asked me if I wasn't afraid
he'd poke my eyes out, but a moment later he burst into
tears and begged me not to take you away. As for you, you
didn't even say good-bye to him—which didn't surprise me.
Then another home, a theft, and the reformatory. When you
got out, you took up with a ship's officer and shared his bed
for a whole winter. When I went to see you at his place, you

were punch-drunk from idleness, whiskey, and possibly from the sailor's tropical yarns. For want of a better solution, I left you there. But when April came, and with it the shipping season, the sailor went to sea after regretfully kicking you out—his apartment was full of Oriental bric-a-brac, so of course he had to lock it up.

You told me all this later on in a letter with little drawings attached. After the departing sailor you drew the aging conjuror with the bow tie, whose factotum you became, and the decrepit half-ton truck in which you toured the provinces together. In the margin you sketched your props: the fringed top hat, the egg with a hole in it, the mangy rabbit, the pack of cards, the three ivory balls, and the magic wand you placed in the master's rheumatic hand on the stages of village cultural centers. If his tricks were a flop, you did handstands, turned cartwheels, showed your thighs, and sang a song about an old-time brothel to entertain the small but demanding audience. At night you slept together on damp peasant beds, but sometimes the village dignitaries invited you, without your partner, to dine on pheasant or venison in the hunting room of the local inn, and then you were late in getting home. "When I come in," you wrote, "my old man is always crying into the pillow. But that doesn't prevent him from asking me for money to buy gas and rent the next hall." In mid-autumn the audience took exception to your pregnant cartwheels. As you told me in a letter, you didn't know who the father was. The question lost its relevance, at least from the child's point of view, when the conjuror, exhausted by love, began to foam at the mouth and gasp for air. You somehow loaded the old man into the spluttering truck and delivered him to the district hospital; then, without waiting to see if he would recover or remain an invalid, you abandoned truck, rabbit, top hat, the whole works, at the hospital gate, caught a train, and turned up at my office, to see what I might suggest. By then you were of age and I would have sent you packing, but your bulging stomach made you a client again. That's when I got you the room you have now. When your son was born, I took him into official custody, at your request writing in the "profession of the putative father" blank: University Professor.

I recommended you to restaurants. This is the fifth. I knew that the imitation wine barrels they use for chairs, the candles weeping into wrought-iron saucers, the barbecue, the red lamps, and the fake timber beams would appeal to you; and I also guessed that at closing time, befuddled by muscatel, you would stop at the corner if a customer was waiting, and take his arm.

I only wanted to find you a place to live, and quite by chance it turned out to be here. It was strange to think of you under one roof with Bandula. Bandula with his frightened sense of justice and the humiliated longing for freedom in his shoe-button eyes, you with your two heavy breasts, a handful. You would let him whimper outside your door that you opened to everyone else—perhaps because of the dim-witted child, or the vague presence of his wife in the other room, or, most probably, because of his biting servility; you would have kicked him in the ribs rather than say: "Go take a bath and I'll let you in." Once he told me he used to look through your keyhole when you were making love. And you yourself told me without anger that you kept hearing him panting out there. You could have let him in just once. Even a frail branch can catch a suicide in his fall.

3

I put on the light and leave the door open. Anna comes along, followed by a bald, guffawing customer with big ears. Under each arm he is carrying a long-necked bottle; he aims one of them at me, saying: "Bang! Pay up and you

151

can come along, fifty-fifty." Anna says nothing, neither do
I; he explains how we can share her, who will begin where,
we're pals, aren't we? He pushes his way in, puts his big
hand on Feri's head, and tells us how one winter he took
two girls to the park so one could lie down in the snow and
he could lie on top of her with the other. He smacks the
bottom of one bottle with his open palm and the cork pops
out. Anna tells him to go away; he refuses, but then she
gives him a girl friend's address with a note. Yes, she's a
redhead with a big behind and a thin waist. She charges
less, it's on the next street. She can bring in a friend if he
wants a threesome. What about the wine? I pay him for the
opened bottle. He gives me his visiting card; I should go
out with him sometime, he knows a place where we can pick
up some good ass. Everybody likes him because he's a regular guy. He points the other bottle at me, "bang!" pushes
his black-ribboned straw hat down over his ears, guffaws,
and vanishes down the corridor.

I tell Anna what I want; she drinks and says nothing,
except to invite me to supper. She straightens the child's
bed and covers him. "I was thinking," I say, "of giving up
my job and moving in here to look after the child, but then
this solution occurred to me." She's pleased, but doesn't see
why I should give up my job. I should go on working, she'd
look after the child and bring home her own; the four of us
would live together. "How stupid I've been," I say. "When
it was all so simple." What about my family? she asks.
Do I want to leave home? "No, I wouldn't have left if it
hadn't been for the child." In that case I should stay home,
but I might as well spend the night with her; she'd look
after the child till there was room for it in an institution.
"They're expecting me home," I say, "I'd better go. I was
going to take him for tonight, but if it's all right with you,
I'll leave him here." All right, she says, but we could finish
off the wine in her room. Her bed is covered with a bearskin; she sits me down on it. She fills two tall wine glasses

152

and says: "Let's go to bed, we've both earned it." "We certainly have," I say, "but as long as we've never got around to it yet, let's not do it now—no use mixing things." She unbuttons her dress and presses up against me. I'd like to bite her, but I don't; it would be only a conditioned reflex. She runs her hand through my hair. When I open my eyes, she's buttoning up again. "Could you make love to me?" I nod. "But you don't want to?" I shake my head. "Next time then," she says, and I stroke her arm. "But about the child," I say. "You'll take him anyway for a few weeks, won't you?" "I've already said I would—for free, I don't want you to pay me." She tells me that she cried over Bandula. She has a picture of him. She's going to pin it up on the wall; he was a good man. I get up from the bearskin. "You're good, too," I say. "I'm a whore." "Doesn't mean a thing, we're all of us whores." I wouldn't mind another drop of wine, but I pick up my briefcase and open the door. The child is asleep in there, now there's someone to look after him.

THE COMPANY
OF THE NAMELESS

On the deserted square the steps of late passers-by stand out sharply from all other sounds. The last audience has poured out of the movie house, passing from torrid darkness into the cool night air; parched and silent, they scatter and vanish into the eight streets leading out of the square. The market building with its burned brick bastions grows in the milky light of the vapor lamps. I cross the road and walk past the stacked crates and corded baskets, the canvas tarps held down by bricks, the nylon covers draped over heaps of beets and turnips. I pass the fisherwomen dozing on crates and sacks (lying on their sides with their knees drawn up, face to face in pairs, they look like squat bundles, very different from the porters sprawled immodestly on their carts). The stalls, so flourishing in the daytime, have removed their masks; planks, stakes, iron frames, benches, and trestles lie chained together on four-wheeled hand trucks. I pass between chickens sleeping in their coops and piles of wilting, pungent-smelling cabbage, step across the swaying, rectangular shadow of the night watchman making his rounds, leaving behind me the solemn rank—interspersed with magnolias, carnations, and white funeral wreaths—of foodstuffs classified according to nature and kind, of rotting, oozing, stinking foodstuffs. Turning back on this moon-drenched arena of rhythmic consumption, of pulsating intake and output, I freely select one of the eight possible streets branching off from the square. A few steps further on, perhaps from fatigue, I am overcome by dizziness. I stop and steady myself against a pile of planks. I turn around and look for a lighted window on the other side of the square under a foliate cornice (if I remember right). A female silhouette is framed in the light. My eyes shift to a dark window behind which, earlier this evening, in peacetime, I held the hand of an idiot boy, and tried secretly to go over to the other side.

2

Evening surrenders to night, and the street to the hour of my homecoming. The afternoon shift discharges hairdressers, waitresses, cashiers, cleaning women, female coilwinders, polishers, glassblowers, computer card punchers, ushers, packers, and dishwashers. They trip along on iron-edged heels, flap along in thonged sandals, bound along in soft moccasins, stamp along in high-laced boots; and close on their heels, on rubber soles, armed with transistors and crumpled movie guides, comes the morose, determined throng of ironworkers and roofers, warehousemen and crane operators, grocery clerks, coal heavers, and car washers; they overtake the women, look around, wait, mark time in front of drab shop windows, fall back and surge forward, swing from one sidewalk to the other, from one side street to another, light cigarettes, and rush on. Each indicating his property right by following his chosen victim at an interval of five paces, they pursue the stream of tired, potato-chip munching, window-gazing, hair-patting, string-bag toting, humming, ill-made-up women. Suddenly one bridges the gap, says a few words, and the two go on together; or after a sentence or two, the man turns aside with a look of misplaced pride, and a moment later he is following another figure. Thrusting their left hands into their trouser pockets, the memory of their setbacks frozen on their faces, gradually losing hope of a quick and satisfactory solution, ready to accept anything because the day is over and nothing has happened, because of all possible events this is the only one to clutch hold of, they plod homeward, dreading the moment when the front door will close behind them, dreading the sultry night in their furnished rooms, the clammy contact of an all-too-familiar foot; on they plod toward an unfastening of buttons and zippers, an unhooked brassière, rolled-down stockings, breasts the size of a baby's head, buttocks overwrought with legends of adolescence, toward an all-engulfing vulva, an ineffable wedding night, an orgy of flesh, skin, and hair, a sculptural emblem of passion, intoxication, abandon; on they plod toward an attic, a basement, a rancid-smelling cubicle, the dark back room of some shop, a dank pit full of oil barrels; on they plod until their swollen feet and aching backs make it clear to them that they desire nothing more—only to sleep.

156

In the picture framer's window a pink-faced, cherry-mouthed Saviour, with silky, blond permanent-waved hair fenced around by a forest of thorns, looks heavenward; at his feet, the three inevitable bears on a fallen pine trunk and my fragmented face in a gilt-framed, coffin-shaped mirror in a dawn the color of apricot jam; a black brook wends its way through frost-white woods; dogs in evening dress stand about with horsewhips in their hands and spectacles on their noses, a lion in a bridal veil sits smiling under a tiny gas lamp, a mechanical man in a gilt miter plays the saxophone alongside his spaceship; not far off I glimpse the imperishable birthday cake topped with a hatted rabbit, a dancing duck, and birthday greetings inscribed in sugar substitute; and in another corner, surrounded by the blown-up faces of pop singers and football players, a stylized Lenin with fist-sized cheekbones and sky-scraping skull. I can't take my eyes off the weird war machines, the red, tinkling, remote-controlled tank, the rattling, flashing machine gun, the rubber-band-propelled rocket mounted on an eight-wheeled truck, the little yellow plastic soldiers preparing to throw hand grenades or lunging at dark-blue plastic soldiers with old-fashioned bayonets. With the wonderment of rediscovery, I look at the emblems of our ecstasies and enchantments, our festive moments and longings, our omniscience and our competitive fervor. I make my way past the small workshops of dental technicians and tailors and fountain-pen repairers, of tombstone, plastic-flower, wig, and fur-slipper makers, chiropodists, and costume renters. I take in a half-nude Virgin wearing the firebrands of her heart on her sleeve, a cancan dancer in a lace skirt and carmine panties on top of a cupboard between two jars of cherry preserves, six honey-colored coils of fly-paper dangling flyless from the six arms of a fake Venetian chandelier, a snow-white crown of hair, a crutch propped against a green-shimmering aquarium, enlarged family photographs (the children squatting in front, the grandparents sitting bolt upright on chairs, behind them the parents, hatted or unhatted—the pillars of continuity), a grimy wall with telegrams of condolence pinned to it, a hussar marching out of a grandfather clock painted in the national colors and waiting with one foot upraised for the time to go back in. Shaking myself free from this vision of a sleazy baroque world of which I myself am a part, I trudge down one of the eight side streets leading out of the square.

4

Slowly, challengingly, an empty taxi moves past; nobody hails it. Passing the iron-barred windows of the vivisection laboratories, I hold my breath; I am only too familiar with the smell of dissected rats. Farther on, I peer back at the trail of chalk footsteps behind me. Someone might be following me. I wouldn't mind in the least if an indignant censor of morals were to approach and demand an explanation of my misdeeds. I could go on explaining until he reached retirement age; then he would entrust the investigation to someone else, whom I would likewise wear down.

In a cramped yellow streetcar sits a scrawny conductress with a pocket mirror, masking her nascent wrinkles with makeup. I ought to reassure her, tell her she has picked the right color; I only give her an approving nod; she gives me a surprised glance and turns back to her mirror. Outside the padlocked cellar door leading down to the Assembly of the Living God two urchins are fencing with iron rods; one of them stamps his foot and presses his advantage, the other pants and drops his rod. Nasty little brats. Whether I like it or not, my working time is theirs; sometimes I feel friendly to them and would do almost anything for them, but I refuse to worry about their futures. God forbid that they should become an obsession with me. We're strangers; I do my part, the rest is up to them.

A teen-ager in a leather jacket grabs hold of a girl and pulls her back by the forehead for his friend to kiss her. Two diminutive boys go past and look back disapprovingly; the girl bursts out laughing. In a lighted basement three Gypsies squat on beds that have been pushed together. In front of them a long-necked young woman in a white lace dress poses like a model. The young men nod and a brown hand draws the curtain.

A shower of sparks from a passing streetcar picks out a nineteenth-century wall, blackened with smoke and marked by rain, frost, and history. Some time ago, quite a long time ago now, a young girl was standing against this wall. Concealed in a doorway not far off, her father was waiting for her, but the girl was already dead. The bullets that passed through her body riveted her burned coat to the plaster. When her father ventured out and tore her away from the wall, she fell on him. He held her for a while, then laid her down on the sidewalk. Behind the wall, the high-ceilinged rooms are sometimes full to overflowing with the memory-less present. In a lighted room two girls in nightgowns are playing with a brightly colored beach ball. The ball floats at irregular intervals from the brightness of one window to the brightness of the other, from a still life with roses to a still life with fishes.

At the terminus a man in his fifties helps a middle-aged woman onto a bus, but doesn't get on himself. The woman stands on the rear platform looking out the window, smiling like someone who has received an unexpected birthday card. The man looks at her through thick spectacles, and when the bus moves off, he waves. Another bus arrives from the opposite direction. When all the passengers have gotten off, the conductress gets down from behind her collecting box, kneels on the front seat, pushes back the window to the driver's cab, leans forward, and kisses the cigarette-smoking driver on the ear.

I could never be a statesman, priest, or believer, the historical and divine pretenses at brotherhood simply baffle me. Nevertheless, in my present no man's land between little Bandula, who is now off my hands, and my family, to whom I have not yet returned, I search for my fellow man, always certain that the chosen one, my brother, is the one who happens to be coming toward me. I am incapable of addressing him by name, but he is not unknown to me. I watch him as he passes, and because I have noticed him, he takes me with him. Now and then my brother stops me and asks me for a light. In some of my modest metaworlds I live and die barely as long as it takes me to strike a match and look him in the face; in others it takes longer.

Under the chestnut trees in the rhomboid square old ladies are sitting on benches in groups of four. Some are knitting or reading by the light of the street lamps; most of them are doing nothing. They have company at their elbows, and at least they're not wasting electricity at home. Passing one of the benches, I see four small immobile, yellowish knots of hair. In their laps the ladies have ancient handbags, open letters, and canes with gleaming metal handles. With an expression of vacant anxiety they watch the passers-by, most of whom look away. I am reminded of the three bedridden, mentally atrophied old women unable to speak, eat, or go to the toilet, who reacted to no stimulus of any kind, but simply looked at each other, smiling continually for years on end.

Two boys are sitting straddle-legged on a bench, playing chess under the street lamp. At brief intervals, one or the other strikes one of the two knobs of the timer they have placed on a pile of bricks beside them. Some men are standing around them with folded arms, rubbing their chins in taut silence. Presently one boy says, "Well, that's it!" The other sweeps the pieces into a box and takes the timer under his arm; they shake hands and set off in different directions.

I need another drink. The iron shutter has already been lowered outside one bar, but the next is still open. Two brownish-red cripples are guarding the swinging door with the matter-of-factness of customs officers, barring the way with their crutches. They won't get a drink out of me. I stand with my glass by the blind piano tuner, who shakes his pale face and complains to his friend: "I've got worries and troubles, heaps and heaps of troubles. You're not the only pebble on the beach. Remember that now and then." They embrace, then grapple with each other. "If it's a point of honor, leave me out of it," growls a coal heaver over three plates of stew. The stew has its admirers, two turkey-necked old men's lower lips tremble, the old woman is singing a song about her dead mother. At the other bar two young men try to put a fur cap on another young man's head, but he pushes them away and throws the cap on the floor. A sailor with a white collar asks a big-breasted waitress if he can sleep with her tonight. The woman sticks her head in the serving hatch, showing him her rear end, but the sailor stands patiently, and when the woman turns, surprised to see him still there, he asks again if he can sleep with her tonight. One of the staff appears in lavender overalls and jockey cap and starts thumping the stone floor with a long, hooked iron rod. The customers protest and abuse him, but Jockey Cap keeps thumping, and the bartender bellows, "For Chrissake hurry up and geddout, we're closin'." An old woman in boots is already slopping bucketfuls of gray, soapy hot water on the stone floor. Tonight is over.

5

I cut across the square and give a cigarette to a drunkard who is clutching a lamp post. He steps over the chain separating the sidewalk from the roadway and drifts diagonally across the street. A car bumper grazes his trouser leg, but he manages to reach the gutter, carefully gets down on his hands and knees, and vomits into it. I enjoy watching the steady, phased movement of cars through the gas station, from gas pump to oil rack to air pump, and the gleam of stop lights on the windshield of the car behind. I wait dutifully for the double clang of a streetcar about to enter the depot and the buzz of its warning light; then I cross over, make use of the public toilet, get a pack of cigarettes and a telephone slug from a slot machine, and call up my home from a telephone booth. Within the glass cylinder, my shoulders suddenly fall forward from fatigue. For a few seconds I listen to my wife's hellos, then I remember to press the red button. Yes, I'll be home in half an hour, yes, it has really been quite a long day, no, there's nothing wrong, darling, the usual sort of thing, I've been kind of snowed under. I scrape my nail up and down over the coin slot, fidget with the dial. I almost brought a child home with me. What child? A bit odd, but nice. No, I've decided not to, yes, of course I'm coming. Tomorrow I'll be home on time, we won't be late for the movies. The younger one's got a cough, you say? Has he caught cold? Thanks for waiting, I'll be home in three-quarters of an hour at the most.

On the other end of the sidewalk I pass a file of taxis turning into the station; the Vienna train will be leaving in half an hour.

On the wall of the ticket hall, seaside hotels, beach umbrellas of every color, sunbathers stretched out on the sand, small heads bobbing up and down in the water. Holding ragged cigarettes between their stubby fingers, suburban workers on their way home after the afternoon shift are gaping at posters featuring ancient Greek aqueducts, Roman arches, and Turkish mosques. A local is about to leave on Track 4, all aboard and please shut the doors. Red stockings, red dresses, black cloaks, black hats, white-painted mouths, green eye shadow, dogs, porters, relatives, "I'll send you the dresses." Dog-faced gold goblets, silver anklets, malachite rouge pots, dragonhead earrings, ornamental daggers, death masks, and figurines from the tombs of the pharaohs. Soldiers on the way back to their units look at the pictures. A peasant boy with sideburns and bell-bottoms walks out of Men Messieurs Muzsscin Herren, nonchalantly buttoning his fly. On a shelf an excursion boat lit up with fairy lights is waiting to be launched. An auxiliary policeman picks out a saddle-nosed, fluffy-haired woman and asks for her papers, but she spits and scurries away in the crowd; a uniformed policeman who happens to be standing by the door stops her, and she promptly pulls out her identity card. Brand-new coking plants, oil refineries, rolling mills, tube mills, labyrinthine cable-car systems crisscrossing in every direction, cylindrical buildings, streamlined skyscrapers, metal archways between storage tanks, networks of pipes, towering cranes, wide-span arc-shaped stressed-skin structures, assembly halls resting on light supporting piers. A Gypsy in oil-stained navy-blue overalls, with a dagger at his belt, is carrying a bloody lamb wrapped in newspaper, its head dangling from his shoulder. In the distance, snow-covered hills, palm-fringed avenues, white fishing vessels in a calm, blue bay. In the waiting room passengers are sprawled on benches and tables. An old man with a new bicycle tire around his neck is resting his forehead on his neatly folded coat while his hand clutches a beer bottle. Three young men are sitting with their heads propped on their shoulders, their hands hanging limply from their

163

raised forearms, their suitcases resting between their knees. In the russet light of Genesis, Dürer's Adam and Eve perform a stately dance, their locks flutter in the breeze, foliage covers their sexual parts, a diminutive snake proffers a gleaming red apple. On one of the wooden tables a blanket is spread out, on top of it a linen sheet, and on the sheet a baby sleeping with its diapers undone; beside the baby sits its young mother, eyeing it gravely. Advertisements for skin creams, package tours, the latest thing in bathing suits, camping equipment, airlines, and art festivals. At one of the tables in the waiting room an excited old peasant is explaining something to a young woman who is probably his daughter; maybe he wants her to come back to the village—there, too, she can find work. The young woman is bored, she twists her ungainly signet ring, and slips the shoe off her swollen right foot. She stares at the pictures of primeval reptiles, mammoths, giant whales, and folk costumes on the wall, her eyes flit over the production graph and settles on advertisements for beauty salons, mountain hotels, beachwear, waterproof tents, bus tours, and open-air theaters.

The express stopped at the village station for only thirty seconds; only five or six people got off, but even so it was worthwhile to go and meet it. I picked out a face behind the glass and accompanied him to his unknown destination. I've taken trains, I know how the traveler, slumped in the seat, looks out wearily at the passing telegraph poles and the locals loafing about at the stations. I put on this face chosen at random, this forehead leaning against the bluish windowpane of an international express. By tomorrow several frontiers will have closed behind him; thanks to various forms (please attach recent photo here) and the power of the rubber stamp, he has acquired the right to be saluted by official caps of varying shapes and sizes. He will take in the black cows, the white churches, the chairman of the board telephoning from his car, the Negro nun on a motor bike, the traffic being directed from a helicopter, the two hundred twenty-six brassière-clad dummies in the basement of a department store, the whore being pushed away from the pinball machine, the mustachioed Girl Scout leader trudging along the dusty road, the beggar woman whimpering at the feet of a disgusted policeman, the workers drinking soberly in the café, telling each other what they had to eat on their summer holidays. He, too, will develop a taste for spider crab, crayfish, lobster, duck with bamboo shoots, and *coq au vin*, and one afternoon in early fall he will stretch out on the pebbly beach, with an unprecedented sense of peace, far from the herd of routine-ridden gargoyles, far from the red-, blue-, or silver-gleaming nuclear complex, under the wheeling gulls, beside him a straw hat sparkling with salt. He will slap the pebbles with a banana skin, and if while he is lying there an anonymous hand were to touch his eyelids and an already familiar voice were to ask in a foreign tongue what he is thinking about, he would answer that he is thinking of nothing, or only that it seems so funny to think of the battered continent behind him; he could easily abandon it altogether, but he won't; he'll spend another few days at the seaside hotel; then, grown sick of the water, the seashells, the fishermen, the Swedish girls who think of nothing but bathing, even of the red wine and onion soup, he will head back to the interior of the continent. When he starts reading the local news in his paper and complaining about the soaring prices, when he leaves his map in the drawer and is able to find his way without asking, when his room has taken on the smell of his skin, tobacco, and toilet articles, when in the subway station he tries for the third time to insert the blind Chinaman's money into the orange-juice slot of the vending machine, when he gets back into the habit of standing in line in the dark, vaulted corridors of public buildings, not daring to tell the pipe-smoking, ear-scratching clerk that he has been waiting a long, long time to get that document stamped, then, I should say, there will no longer be much difference between us; he could just as well be me, standing here shortly before midnight as the crowd thins at the outgoing-trains end of a dismal, old-fashioned railroad station, after a similar, though perhaps somewhat more tiring day in one of this battered continent's cities, a city to which—with half of our lives behind us—we are inexorably bound by habit.

INVITATION

And so tomorrow, and for another twenty-odd years, I shall squeeze through the heavy iron gate at half-past eight in the morning, make my way between the prying eyes of the porter and the wall with its memorial plaques. The elevator, warmed by its infrared heater and my work-bound colleagues, will carry me to the fourth floor, where I shall press the handle, sticky from the touch of innumerable hands, of the door that bears my nameplate. The years have worked their slow ravages on the furnishings and equipment listed in the inventory, but also on the unlisted items that help to people the room: the increasingly suspect relations between the filing cabinet and the petrified destinies inside it, between the indestructible Remington and my disintegrating features, between the leather sofa—a relic of the imperial bureaucracy and still in good condition—and the associations I have buried in its depths.

I question, explain, prove, disprove, comfort, threaten, grant, deny, demand, approve, legalize, rescind. In the name of legal principles and provisions I defend law and order for want of anything better to do. The order I defend is brutal though fragile, it is unpleasant and austere; its ideas are impoverished and its style is lacking in grace. I can't pretend to like it. Yet I serve it, it's law, it works, it's rather like me, its tool. I know its ins and outs. I simplify it and complicate it, I slow it down and speed it up, I adapt myself to its needs or adapt it to my needs, but this is as far as I will go. I repudiate the heroes of the Fresh Start, with their pedantic recommendations and mawkish visions; I repudiate their blueprints for a *perpetuum mobile*, which for the time being (but only for the time being) has to be started with a crank and operated under the strictest supervision. I repudiate the high priests of individual salvation and the sob sisters of altruism, who exchange commonplace partial responsibility for the aesthetic transports of cosmohistorical guilt or the gratuitous slogans of universal love. I refuse to emulate these Sunday-school clowns and prefer—I know my limitations—to be the skeptical bureaucrat that I am. My highest aspiration is that a medium-rank, utterly insignificant civil servant should, as far as possible, live with his eyes open.

In the meantime, my belly swells, my legs turn spindly, my mouth fills with gold, the hair on the back of my hands goes white, the perenniality of human failure grinds me and consumes me. I shuffle back and forth between tottering stacks of paper, I move eternally pending files from drawer to drawer and shelf to shelf, I turn into a cantankerous old bureaucrat who locks up his rubber stamp when he goes to the toilet, and refuses to lend anyone his book of regulations. I write my memos in a smaller and smaller hand on slips of paper cut out with my pocketknife. I cite my age and experience, time and time again I repeat the same anecdotes and words of advice, I get my clients mixed up, doze off more and more often while listening to them. I snap at them if they interrupt me or talk too much, I dismiss their complaints, and if any of them bursts into tears, I suck furiously on my cheap, foul-smelling cigar.

2

In the meantime I wait for my clients. Let the children— our examiners—come with their hot hands and fragrant round heads, their laced shoes that swing like pendulums, and the smiles they display like medals, their atavistic fears and amazing ability to learn, their obsessions and cajoleries, their relentless selfishness and irresistible weakness, their vulnerable docility and their mirror images of our own depravity . . .

let all the children come, the babies abandoned in hospitals and nurseries, in doctors' offices and on strangers' laps, on park benches and in garbage cans, the chilled, the urine-soaked, the withered babies left choking under pillows, rescued from gas-filled rooms crushed against the wall, thrown on the ground, abandoned amid broken glass and potato peelings; let them all come, our unbidden, avenging enemies . . .

let children from the institutions come, with their numbered underwear and vacant eyes; all who wait behind bars for visitors who never come, whose tearful, pleading letters never bring an answer, who shrink back from mothers just released from jail, who thrash about with burning paper between their toes and hide their ink-stained genitals, all those who are adopted so they can mind the dog in the daytime and bring the milk from the dairy, and those who look forward to Christmas because a crazy old woman has a few slices of bacon waiting for them in her garret littered with peat and wood shavings . . .

let the runaways come, those caught after nights spent in the woods, in confessionals, cotton bales, sandboxes, or empty pigsties; the boy who is unconsolable because his mother has moved him to the floor to make room in bed for her new lover; the girl who was going to put her half-sister's eye out with a red-hot poker but dropped it at the last minute; the youth whose father chased him around the yard with a knife and had almost caught him when a pious widow next door tripped the father up with her broomstick, pulled the boy in, and laughed and cried, and covered him with kisses while he ate and slept . . .

let all the others come, those whom no amount of candy, tears, and toy trains can keep at home, who climb out the window, toss their school bags into the cellar, hide stolen money under their inner soles, arm themselves with compass, kitchen knife, paper mask, and flashlight, and set out for the border, for new worlds across the sea, but end up in jail, where food is served only every other day; who, when released, hunt down the informer and kick him in the groin; who on a visit home knock down their mothers and take the key to the money box; who jump handcuffed from the train, break through the crowd of curious old people outside the courthouse, and with panting prison guards at their heels, jump onto a passing truck; who crawl through the cornfields of the prison farm to take off their prison uniforms in a ditch; who break out of the cells, scramble over brick walls, and regularly get caught, shivering in a swamp, breaking into weekend cottages, sleeping on a pile of sugar beets in a freight car, or in the bed of a girl friend who turns them in to the police; who finally, enrolled in the ranks of full-fledged convicts, sit gray-haired or bald in their cells or on the tractors in the prison yard, speaking little, possessing nothing worth taking away when they're searched, bursting into tears on the day of their release, when the warden shakes hands with them and wishes them well . . .

let them all come with their manias and threats of vengeance, their porno-collages, their short-wave transmitters hidden in shoe-polish tins, their electrical masturbators, their jars of poisoned jam, their cakes full of pins, nails, and fishbones, their vaginas full of jewelry, and all the rest of their cunning little dodges; let them all come, those who roll their eyes and gnash blackened teeth, who suck their thumbs, bite their nails, and scratch their palms; those who squirt vitriol from water pistols, who tattoo their heads or blow soap bubbles, who smear paint on the window to prevent prying neighbors from looking in, who put buckets over the door to prevent the porter from raping them; those who sew up their pockets with needle and thread every evening to keep their wives from helping themselves, who use a different alias every time you meet them, who write anonymous denunciations of themselves to distract official attention, who tie their daughter to the kitchen table, boil water, and sharpen the bread knife to cut the child of a red-haired Jewish ragpicker out of her belly; all those who will be taught to make paper flowers and be allowed to attend a puppet show once a month, who wait for hypothetical visitors behind white doors that can be opened only from the outside, who stand in striped nightshirts among therapeutic potted plants and piles of embroidered tablecloths, or roam about, careful to step only in certain squares of the parquet floors, until at last their relatives, notified by a letter typed on cheap, absorbent paper, call for them or for their knitted jackets and wedding rings . . .

let the tyrants of selfishness come, with all their manias

and deadly, futile wrongs; those who rage on the telephone because they can't get through, those who wallow in excuses, the secret judges who can never acquit themselves, the martyrs who ultimately die of some comic misunderstanding, the leeches and hamsters of love, the shivering outcasts, the lepers whose birthday no one remembers, those who when embraced in front feel lonely behind, whose bright new penny always gets stolen by a magpie . . .

let the eternal underdogs come, those whose ribs are crushed year in year out by the same steel spring, whom conjugal love prevents from stretching their legs, who have never had as much room as a convict in a humane prison system, who hold their breath when they copulate, who through their cellar windows see only the shoes of their fellow creatures, who are never alone except in their fourth-rate coffins, those around whom iron turns to rust, plaster crumbles, wood rots, cloth grows threadbare, the window mists over and cracks. Processions sometimes start out from such homes. Out marches the Sunday best, along with the sheets and pillowcases; summer clothes in the winter, overcoats in the summer; pictures of the Virgin fly off the walls, china dogs run away, the radio backs out through the door, followed by the tablecloth. The shelves empty, the mattresses strip, the wires run out of electricity, and then the furniture begins to move out with a slow, bumping gait . . .

let the bungling mechanics come, those who can never put themselves together out of their component bits and pieces, who can never be real for want of a shirt button, a telephone token, or an aspirin, the neglected who have never been given anything for nothing, the underprivileged whose wildest dream it is to be next to the last, those who live with their backs to the wall, always looking for a place to hide, cringing before they are threatened, those who cannot even be sure their mothers will recognize them tomorrow, those who shuffle from one foot to the other and finally decide not to ring the bell after all, those with trembling lips who are never let in on the secret, those who don't write that letter because they can't make up their minds how to address the recipient, those who never get picked for either team in the school playground, whose hats always get sat on, those who walk straight into every flying gob of spit, apple core, or burning cigarette butt, those who get the leftover pudding or wife, who bathe, dust, and copulate once a week, who are always being asked how they are by people who are already walking away, who often cry into mirrors, who see the silver angels of cathedral altars on sunlit alley walls, who, wavering between disgust and indifference born of familiarity, can, in a privileged moment of tenderness, light the Christmas sparkler of mescaline-induced recognition and exalt the law of inalienable freedom above the experience of their own insignificance . . .

let all those come who want to; one of us will talk, the other will listen; at least we shall be together.